BORDER
LEGEND
TRILOGY

SPANISH EYES

LEE BISHOP

This is a work of fiction. Names, characters, places, and incidents are products of the author's imagination or are used fictitiously and are not to be construed as real. Any resemblance to actual events, locations, organizations, or persons, living or dead, is entirely coincidental.

World Castle Publishing, LLC
Pensacola, Florida
Copyright © Lee Bishop 2016
Paperback ISBN: 9781629894935
eBook ISBN: 9781629894942
First Edition World Castle Publishing, LLC, July 18, 2016
http://www.worldcastlepublishing.com
Licensing Notes
Cover: Karen Fuller
Editor: Maxine Bringenberg

DEDICATION

This novel is dedicated to my wife, Sue, to whom I dedicate all my novels. I've had the pleasure of being married to this wonderful woman for more than thirty years.

CHAPTER 1

Carmen Rodriguez stopped hanging laundry on the line outside the small adobe house and studied three horsemen riding towards her through the golden, knee-high grass. She suddenly felt ill at ease, not recognizing the men as being cowboys from the Barringer Ranch, and turned her head, eyes searching the grasslands behind her for her husband, Paco.

***

Larry "Patch" O'Brien, a railroad foreman, stopped his horse in front of the pretty brunette and his companions did the same. A black patch covered his right eye, the result of a bar fight that had gone bad years earlier. "We need water," he stated in a hard voice as he surveyed the prairie, not seeing anyone near the line house ten miles from the main ranch complex.

Carmen pointed to a well about fifty yards away. "Take as much as you want," she replied. The young woman felt a cold chill come over her. "My husband will be back in a few minutes."

"What's a sweet thing like you doin' out here?" the second man, Red Drago, asked. A hawk-like nose and small mouth gave him the look of a rat. His shifty, dark eyes continually moved up and down Carmen's body.

O'Brien and Drago dismounted and approached Carmen, who was suddenly terrified, eyes wide and mouth open. A smirk spread across O'Brien's square, block-like face as he reached out and grabbed Carmen's arm. Drago grabbed her other arm as she began screaming, twisting, trying to break free.

"All we want is a good time. Stop fighting, it won't do you no good," said the reddish-blond-haired enforcer who inflicted harsh punishment at the bidding of the Central Pacific Railroad foreman.

O'Brien ripped the front of her dress from the neck down to her waist, and the two men began laughing excitedly as if they were playing a game. The third rider, a seventeen-year-old boy, Tim Edwards, had a look of horror on his face as the assault and rape unfolded. "No!" he cried out. "What are you doing?"

Carmen's screams brought her husband on the run from the arroyo he had been clearing of debris. He carried a machete and began yelling as the two men pulled Carmen into the small house. Paco ran by Edwards, who was still on his horse, and plunged through the doorway, machete raised, ready to strike O'Brien.

"Get away from her, leave my wife alone!" he shouted. Drago shot the slender young man through the heart, and he fell dead with an incredulous look frozen on his face. Carmen was screaming hysterically as she pulled free from her assailants and rushed to her husband's side, throwing her arms around Paco.

"I didn't see him comin'," O'Brien observed.

"He's just a Mex," Drago replied. "Shall we finish what

we came here to do?"

"Might as well," said the railroad foreman, renowned for his cruel, violent treatment of railroad workers.

The men grabbed Carmen and dragged her kicking and screaming to the bed. Drago, an enforcer who specialized in savage beatings and murder when needed, slapped Carmen hard across the face, almost knocking her unconscious.

***

Outside, Tim Edwards dismounted and fell to his knees as the screaming began again, his mouth open, a terrified look on his face. The young man was O'Brien's courier between job sites and the main railroad office in Tucson, and had never been involved in savagery of any kind. He ran into the grass covered prairie far enough that the young woman's cries and pleadings could not be heard.

***

A half hour later, O'Brien and Drago emerged from the adobe home. The railroad foreman looked around for Edwards. "Tim, where the hell are you!" he yelled. Edwards came stumbling through the grass, white-faced and fearful, his sandy, shoulder-length hair blowing about his slender face.

Drago's eyes narrowed as he studied the young man moving towards him. "What about this kid? Will he keep his mouth shut?" Drago asked his boss.

"He'll be okay. He's the best messenger I've ever had. I don't want to lose him," O'Brien proclaimed. "Too bad that Mex came out of nowhere."

"What about her?" Drago asked, and looked knowingly at O'Brien.

"We don't want to leave any witnesses," the foreman growled.

Without another word being spoken, Drago turned and walked back into the house. There was a scream then a shot, and the enforcer reappeared. Edwards began to shake uncontrollably, eyes wide, lips trembling. O'Brien walked to the young man and slapped him across the face. "Get hold of yourself! You're never to talk about this! Is that clear?" O'Brien said gruffly.

Self-preservation kicked in, and Tim had the presence of mind to nod his head in agreement. "I'll never say anything, I promise," Edwards croaked.

CHAPTER 2

Victoria Barringer glided effortlessly into her large office on the main floor of her house, accompanied by her new mining superintendent Tom Donovan. They seated themselves in leather chairs at a small conference table, and Victoria's friendly personality and beautiful smile were captivating.

"Now that you've been on the job a few months, what is your honest opinion of the longevity of these mining claims?" she asked, eyes never leaving Donovan's face.

The white-haired mining superintendent sat back in his chair, momentarily contemplating a reply. "It depends, Victoria. The gold deposits we're mining will last another two years, minimum. I suspect that the small mountain range behind your current operation will yield another gold field, but quite a bit of drilling and testing will be needed before we'll know for sure."

Victoria closely scrutinized his light blue eyes as he talked, satisfied that he was telling the truth. "Whatever you want, Tom, just let me know. We'll move forward with the testing as quickly as you think it's feasible. Not to change the subject, but I'm curious as to why you would leave the Sacramento area to come here. That's a huge gold field market."

Donovan frowned and exhaled sharply. "My wife died more than a year ago, and I know I didn't spend enough time with her. I was always working, spending at least twelve hours a day at the mine or examining other potential sites. It's a mad house in the California gold fields. I wanted a change, and this seemed like a great opportunity to begin living a normal life again."

Victoria's expression softened and she smiled. "My late husband felt the same way, and told me many times he was sorry for not spending more time with me and the children. I understood and accepted his long hours away from home. Don't be too hard on yourself, women understand."

Although a grandmother, Victoria was still very attractive. Her oval face was accented by high cheek bones, a petite nose, and a lovely complexion. Her regal demeanor and self-assured mannerisms never wavered, but she could be deceptively charming.

"Thanks, I appreciate hearing that from you," Donovan responded. "You told me basically what happened regarding my predecessor. But at the mine I hear various stories. Could you more thoroughly explain the circumstances, if I'm not being too forward?"

"You're not being too forward at all," she replied, smiling as if she was about to discuss a happy occasion. "A mining employee came to me and said Carl Yates and his assistant, Brian Teeter, were skimming large amounts of gold on a monthly basis. I confronted Yates and Teeter in this office, and they drew weapons and made me a captive. They took me to the mine and demanded two hundred thousand dollars in exchange for my release. My grandson, James, did not believe they would allow me to live and staged a daring rescue. Teeter was killed during the rescue and Yates was taken prisoner. I picked up a revolver and shot Yates through the head. No man kidnaps me and lives to talk about it," she emphasized in a hard tone of voice, blue eyes suddenly cold and calculating.

Donovan's eyes widened and his mouth opened, but no words came out. "I didn't mean to pry," he finally uttered, seeming shocked that such a beautiful, sophisticated woman would resort to violence.

Victoria realized that her revelation astounded Donovan, but she had made her point. "You certainly have a right to know the truth since you've taken Yates's place," she assured him, her demeanor returning to that of a benevolent matriarch. She smiled, dazzling white teeth and bright blue eyes transforming her once again into a charming lady.

James Barringer knocked, entered the office, and shook hands with Donovan. "It's good to see you again," said Victoria's tall, handsome grandson. They discussed mining business for the next half hour before Donovan departed.

Victoria studied James, noting that he appeared more cheerful and upbeat. "You seem to be in a good mood today."

The curly-haired general manager was tall, had a broad face, ruggedly handsome features, and a dark tan from being on the range day after day. "I'm enjoying running the ranch. It's almost like I'm managing the Salazar rancho again. Plus, time has eased the disappointment concerning Maria."

James had returned to the Barringer Ranch six months earlier after his marriage proposal to Maria Bustamante had been rejected. James had been raised as Ricardo Montoya in Mexico, and did not learn of his true heritage until his Mexican father, Gustavo, was on his death bed. He told Ricardo he had viewed a stage coach ambush in the Arizona Territory and saw where his real mother had hidden her baby in the rocks.

11

Gustavo rescued the child and took him to Mexico to be raised as his own son. After that revelation, dual identities of Ricardo Montoya and James Barringer would follow him throughout his life.

"I didn't tell you much about what happened in Mexico except that she had said no. It was too painful," he admitted. "But now I do want to explain further."

Victoria did not reply and waited for him to continue.

"At that time, the most important thing in my life was to get Maria Bustamante to marry me," he said and sighed. "She told me that she did not want to marry a man with my lifestyle. She said she wanted a different type of man, a safe man who would be around to raise her children. She said she didn't think I would live that long."

"Those were harsh words," Victoria said in a quiet voice. She stared at her grandson as he reviewed those painful moments in his mind. *He looks as if he's lost somewhere in space*, she thought. "Can we talk some about your trip to Hermosillo?" she asked quietly, thinking it was necessary to change the subject.

His attention snapped back to the present. "I'm sorry, Grandmother. I was reliving the past events, and it still hurts. But if she couldn't accept me for who I am, it probably would not have worked out."

"I have always accepted you for the man you are. You and I are much alike," Victoria declared. "Even though we may want to change, it's doubtful we ever will. We live our lives according to our own code of ethics, our own beliefs in what is right and wrong, and that's all we can do. There's very little justice along the border between the Arizona Territory and Mexico. We both try to make life better for those around us. I use money and influence. You use the gun when necessary."

***

James Barringer, the man with two names and two legacies, smiled. "It's good to hear you say that. You're not playing me like a pawn in a chess game, are you?" he asked jokingly.

Victoria smiled, her expression demonstrating genuine affection for her grandson. "No. I really mean what I say. It's good having you here. You've brought leadership and stability that we have never had for any length of time."

James nodded and smiled. "Let's discuss the Hermosillo trip."

"I want you to go to Hermosillo for two reasons we've discussed before. One is to formalize your Mexican citizenship so you can buy property in Mexico and not be challenged in court. Your Mexican brother, Rafael Montoya, also needs to formalize his citizenship. I realize this process is seldom used because nearly all of the Mexican population is too poor to seek official legalization of their citizenship. Secondly, the two of you are to purchase a medium sized rancho just southeast of the international border to be used as a staging area, so Arizona cowboys can be substituted for Mexican vaqueros on cattle drives north into the Arizona Territory," Victoria noted as she reviewed their earlier conversations.

She continued. "Why do you think Don Jorge Franco is willing to sell his rancho so cheaply? I made him a low offer and he agreed immediately. There has to be a reason."

"My guess is the Apaches. From the information I have been able to obtain, there's a group living in the mountains on the east side of the rancho. If there's been continual raiding, maybe Don Jorge doesn't want to stay."

"Then perhaps we shouldn't purchase it. We can look around for a rancho farther west," Victoria observed.

James thought for a moment. "There are too many unknowns until I have a chance to be on site. One thing we do know is that the rancho is positioned perfectly for how we want to use it. We can even charge Mexican dons for bringing their cattle onto and through our land. They won't complain if it's a reasonable price."

"If we purchase the rancho, do you have an idea how many cattle we can pull together from the open Mexican range land and drive to the border?" she asked.

James fixed his gaze on his grandmother. "There is almost an unlimited number."

Victoria nodded her head. "New United States army posts are springing up all over the southern Arizona Territory. I had a conversation with General Jack Curtis in Tucson not long ago, and he estimated that half of the United States Army soldiers will be in Arizona within a year. Now that the Civil War is over, the army's main job will be to subdue the Apaches. And every post wants beef," she said and smiled. "Let's just briefly go over the issue of stamps of approval again. There are three departments in the Mexican government that must sign off and stamp citizenship papers and contracts. Without all three, the documents are incomplete and therefore not legal."

"I'm not an expert on contracts. Are you sure our interests will be protected?" James asked.

"I've used Mexican attorney Alfredo Garcia on several occasions, and he has proven to be very reliable. I've sent him quite a few clients from the United States, and he wants continuing business from our side of the border."

James nodded his head in understanding.

"I think you will like him. He has a beautiful home and often entertains clients with lavish dinners and parties. He's a man on his way up in Mexican society, and is well thought of in Mexico City," Victoria asserted.

"Suppose I don't understand something in the contract?

Victoria got up from the table and gracefully walked to her desk. She returned with a file. "This is the basic contract in Spanish, and an accompanying deed." She opened the file and turned to a page in the deed that gave all mineral rights to the owner of the property. "Just make sure that the mineral rights in this paragraph are included. We don't want to own the rancho and all of its several thousand acres, and end up with other people mining gold on our land." James took a few minutes to review the contract and deed written in Spanish, set it down, and their eyes met. "You are giving Rafael only forty-nine percent ownership, and fifty-one percent to me."

"That's correct. I want the Barringer family to control the ranch."

James felt anger but did not let it show. "No. You have to understand that this man is my brother. We have been raised together all of our lives, and I trust him with my life. He's an honorable man."

Victoria continued to look James in the eye. "I'm sure he is everything you say he is. But, never let family stand in the way of business."

Well, you never have, James thought to himself. *One of your sons murdered the other, who was my father. I ended up killing the bastard, and was immediately given the job as general manager of the Barringer Ranch and its holdings. Family never gets in the way of business with you.* James shook his head from side to side. "The answer is no. Rafael would feel that I don't trust him, and it would be an insult. I would never do anything to jeopardize our relationship. Also, he would be leaving the Salazar rancho, where he now holds my previous job as segundo. He's the general manager of a much larger ranch than the one we are

15

buying."

Victoria's eyes narrowed. "If I'm not mistaken, you were partially responsible for the death of Don Diego Salazar. Yet, his son, Don Francisco, kept your brother employed at the rancho and promoted him to secondo. He didn't let family get in the way of business."

James sat back in his chair, exhaled sharply, and gathered his thoughts. "There's no way I can win a battle of words with you," he insisted. "But Rafael and I will each have fifty percent ownership in the new rancho. I won't change my position on that point."

Victoria smiled and patted her grandson's hand. "I do admire your character and sense of what is right and wrong. It's what I love about you."

James was perplexed, but her flattering remarks took away some of his anger. "Where is this conversation headed?"

Victoria's calculating expression returned. "All right, it will be a fifty-fifty ownership," she announced. "But, there will be one small codicil or addition to the contract."

"What?" he asked suspiciously.

"In the event that you die, your fifty percent interest in the rancho will revert to Salvador Alhambra," she stated, her eyes sparkling as she spoke.

"Do you mean Sal, the cook?" he asked incredulously.

Victoria laughed. "The head cook here prefers to be called the chef."

James laughed loudly. Victoria controlled all of her employees with strict discipline and regimentation, and Sal jumped at her every request. *He would be the perfect choice to do her bidding*, James thought.

James looked at his grandmother with a respectful gaze. "I suppose we have to have his Mexican citizenship authenticated?"

"I already have the papers drawn up."

James shook his head in wonderment at his grandmother's audacity and ability to anticipate and circumvent business problems, and remain one step ahead of everyone.

"There's one other thing I would like to discuss. While I'm gone, I'd like Silk Mathews to take over my management responsibilities in the field. He has the respect of the cowhands and the ability to lead," James explained.

"You two have become very good friends, and sometimes friendship clouds a person's judgment. Are you sure he's ready for such a broad array of responsibilities?" she asked.

"I'm sure. At times, he has given me advice on how to handle situations differently than I normally would. In other words, he's more diplomatic than I am," James pointed out.

Silk, whose first name was Delbert, had joined the ranch operations more than a year earlier, and instantly impressed James with his skills. He was the finest horseman James had seen, and a top marksman. Because of his thin, blond hair that blew in every direction like corn silk, he was tagged with the nickname Silk at an early age. Mathews was soft-spoken and a gentleman, but the Civil War had forged a toughness in the man that came to the surface in times of conflict.

"I will rely on your judgment. I do like him. He's very intelligent and extremely courteous. And he was with you when the two of you rescued me at the mine," she noted. "What kind of relationship have Silk and William developed?"

William Barringer was James's first cousin, the son of John Barringer, the architect of the ambush that took the lives of James's real mother and father. James killed John Barringer in a knockdown, savage fight to the death. Surprisingly, William appeared relieved that his father was gone, and had become good friends with James. He had been treated with nothing but cruelty by his father throughout his early life, and had hated him.

"William likes Silk's quiet personality and unassuming manner. The two men are very friendly," he told Victoria. "It's a perfect combination of management and accounting."

William had an accounting degree, loved numbers, kept all of the Barringer Ranch's ledgers up-to-date, plus handled banking transactions for the ranch's timber operations, and mining.

The door to the office burst open, and a young Mexican maid stood there crying and trying to talk at the same time. Both Victoria and James sprang to their feet.

CHAPTER 3

"They brought Carmen Rodriguez in...," the young woman cried out. "They raped her and shot her and killed her husband!"

Victoria and James quickly descended the stairs and were directed to one of the guest bedrooms. The Mexican girl lay on the bed, covered with a blanket. The top portion of her head was wrapped in makeshift bandages. Lou Dillard and Dick Abbott, two of the Barringer cowboys, had stopped by the line cabin about an hour after the rape and shootings, and brought Carmen to the main ranch house. She was barely alive from loss of blood. The bullet had not entered her skull, but went along the side of her head.

James turned to the cowboys. "What happened?"

"She was awake some in the back of the buckboard," said Dillard. "Far as I kin tell, three men rode up. They shot Paco, raped her, and then shot her. She said one was very big and had a patch over one eye. The second man had red hair, a long face, and a hook nose. She said he was ugly. The third guy was a young kid, maybe seventeen or eighteen. The kid didn't take part in it."

19

"Dick, find Silk and Cap Ousterhout. Send them here right away. Lou, saddle three horses and bring up three spare horses. Don't saddle my palomino," James ordered.

He put his hand on one of the housemaid's shoulders. "Go to the kitchen and have them put together food for three men for two days."

The young woman looked wide eyed and frightened.

James shook her gently by the shoulder to help her snap out of the trance. "Do it now," he insisted. The girl hurried away.

Dr. Ben Richards arrived a few minutes later and began attending to the young woman, cleaning her wound and applying fresh bandages. Victoria had lured him to live on the Barringer Ranch for twice what he was making from his Tucson medical practice.

After he finished, the white-haired doctor turned to Victoria. "She might make it, but she's lost a lot of blood. It'll depend on whether she wants to live," he emphasized. "I've seen this scenario before. Watching your husband be murdered…it takes a lot out of a person. Sometimes the will to live disappears."

"Well, I know you will do everything you can, Ben," she said.

Silk arrived and Cap Ousterhout was a few minutes behind. James explained to the two men about the rape and murder, and said that the search would begin immediately. Horses were brought to the front of the home, food loaded in saddle bags, and the men prepared to mount just as Victoria emerged from the ranch house. She walked quickly up to her grandson and grabbed his arm.

"Kill the bastards!" she exclaimed, blue eyes hard and unyielding.

Riding away from the Barringer Ranch, James thought that if Victoria had been a man, she would've been just like him.

The three men all looked angry as they approached the small line cabin. James's eyes were mere slits as he dismounted and walked directly inside. Blood was in various locations on the floor and on the bed.

"When we get back, destroy this building," he told Silk. "I don't want anything left to remind me of what took place here." Mathews nodded his head in understanding.

Cap Ousterhout was the best tracker James had worked with. He was old, but still spry for his age, had a grey and white beard that covered his face, a beefy red nose, and brown eyes. A very large stomach resulted in his trousers being held up by suspenders. Chewing tobacco non-stop, Cap walked over to where the three horses had headed north, studied the tracks for a few moments, and shook his head.

"Ain't much ta work with. One horse has a crooked leg, and this makes the horseshoe turn inward. We'll see if we kin still follow it when they join up ta the main road," the old man explained.

A few hours later the men reached the main trail. Cap dismounted and studied the horseshoe prints in the dirt. "I kin still see it. Let's git movin'."

Just before dark, a small trail broke to the northeast. Cap checked the horseshoe prints in the sand.

"Well, that's a break. The turned in shoe print leaves the main trail here, probably headed for Patagonia," Cap noted.

"Should we make camp here and pick up the trail in the morning?" Silk asked.

"Ain't nothing between here and Patagonia. That's where he's headed," said the old man. "If we keep goin' we'll be there by eight or nine o'clock."

James nodded in agreement. "Let's pick up the pace."

The men made good time, stopping only once to switch their saddles on to fresh horses. They continued at a steady pace and reached the small community of about two dozen wooden buildings just after eight o'clock, and stopped in front of a small boarding house that served food. Ralph Bertram, the owner, had various business dealings with Victoria Barringer, and periodically was a guest at the ranch.

"I'll go in first and talk with the owner," James stated. He dismounted, walked up two wooden stairs, and opened the door to the boarding house. No one was visible. James rang a bell on the counter in the front room. Ralph Bertram appeared from a back room and smiled at James. Bertram was in his early forties, bald on top, had a long face, and was very thin.

"What brings you to Patagonia, James?" he asked. The boarding house owner looked closer and saw the steely look in Barringer's eyes.

"We need to talk privately, Ralph," James said quietly.

Bertram motioned for James to come into the back room.

"There was a killing at one of our line cabins. A man was shot to death, his wife raped and then shot in the head and left for dead. Only she didn't die, and she described the murderers."

Bertram's eyes widened and his mouth opened slightly in disbelief. "That's terrible!"

"We think one of the men rode into Patagonia this afternoon. Carmen Rodriguez, the woman who was raped and shot, described the men. One was big and had a patch over one eye. The second man had red hair, a long face, and a hooked nose. She described him as being ugly. The third man was a kid, seventeen or eighteen. Did one of the men matching those descriptions come into Patagonia this afternoon?"

It took Bertram a moment to compose himself and focus on Barringer's question. "The first two men I didn't see ride in, so I doubt that they passed through. The third one, the boy, I think, is staying here. He acted strange, almost detached from what's going on around him. He didn't even come down for dinner. The kid looks terrible. He's waiting for a man named Bob Steele. Steele's a bad one from what I hear, a hired gun."

"What room number?"

"Go upstairs and down the hallway to the last room on the right. It's room 217."

"I've got a couple of men with me. I'll be right back," James said as he turned and walked back outside. Silk and Cap had dismounted and were awaiting instructions.

"It sounds as if the kid is in room 217 upstairs. Silk, you go around to the rear of the building in case he tries to run. Cap, you go inside and sit in one of the chairs in the lobby that gives you a good view of the stairs. Let's go," James emphasized.

Bertram watched from the doorway to the back room as Barringer went quickly up the stairs. "I'd hate to be that kid," he said quietly.

When he reached the room, James listened at the door, but there was no sound. Without trying the door knob, Barringer gave the door a vicious kick and it flew inward. The young man on the bed jumped up into a sitting position, eyes wide, mouth open, and face turning white. The lantern next to the bed cast light across his face, illuminating a terrified expression.

"I know why you're here. Don't kill me! I didn't have anything to do with it, I swear!" he blurted out.

James walked across the room, grabbed the young man by the front of his shirt,
and pulled him off the bed. "You were there when the

23

rape and shootings took place!"

Looking at the anger in Barringer's face, Tim Edwards wore the expression of a man who knew he was going to die. "Please don't kill me...please!" he begged.

"Who were the other two men?" Barringer demanded.

"Patch O'Brien and Red Drago," he said quickly, gasping for breath.

James released the young man's shirt, and Tim almost sank to the ground. "Look. I know you weren't involved. The woman is alive. She told us that it was the other two men. So calm down. I'm not going to kill you. I just want answers to a few questions," James said in a commanding voice.

The boy sank back on the bed. "She's alive? Oh, thank God!" he blurted.

Barringer looked around the room. "Where's your gun?"

"I only have a rifle. It's with my saddle at the stable."

James walked out into the hallway and yelled Cap's name. The old man came running up the stairs, gasping for air from the exertion.

"Get Silk and come here to the room."

An older man across the corridor opened his door. "What's going on here?" he asked in a high-pitched voice.

"Shut up and get back in that room," James told him in a loud voice.

The old man quickly shut his door.

When the three men were assembled a few minutes later, James began questioning Tim Edwards. "Tell me about those two men."

The color had come back into Edwards' face and he looked relieved. "Patch's first name is Larry...no one calls him Patch to his face. He's the foreman for the railroad. O'Brien works those gangs of Chinese and Irishmen until they can barely stand up. But, he always gets the job done on time. They're planning to put a spur railroad line south from Tucson to Nogales."

"What about the man, Red Drago?" Barringer asked.

"He's Patch's top gunman. Whenever Patch needs some dirty work done, he calls on Drago. I hate to be around him. He's as dangerous as a rattlesnake."

"Where will I find him?" James asked.

"He's got a room at the Star Casino Hotel in Tucson. Patch stays in a suite of rooms attached to the railroad headquarters."

Silk spoke for the first time. "Where do you fit into all this?"

"I'm a messenger. I ride wherever Patch tells me to go, deliver messages, and ride back. Its easy work, and I love to ride horses. I'm waiting here for a man named Bob Steele, who I'm supposed to take to Patch."

"Not any more. You're going back to the ranch with Cap. You'll stay there until I return. Is that clear?"

"I wanted to run, but I was afraid they would come after me and kill me. I'm glad you found me. I didn't mean no harm to that man and woman. Please believe me," the young man emphasized, tears in his eyes.

James shifted his gaze to Silk. The tall, blond-haired man shrugged his shoulders. "I think he's telling the truth," Silk observed.

"Cap, keep him on the ranch. We may need him as a witness," James surmised.

The young man appeared confused and frightened. "You mean I might have to testify against Patch and Red?"

"Not hardly. I'm going to kill both of them," James declared in a hard voice.

***

The reality of the situation began to sink in and Tim Edwards' heart sank. If James Barringer was successful, Tim might still be charged with murder. If O'Brien and Drago won out, they would probably kill him. One way or the other, he would face prison or death. His shoulders slumped, his head dropped down, and he felt miserable again.

"My name is James Barringer. The rape and killing occurred on my ranch. Those responsible for it will be brought to justice, and quickly. If you help us, I will see to it that you are treated fairly and won't do any jail time. I want you to go back to the ranch with Cap and stay there until I return. Don't try to leave."

The young man raised his head and felt a glimmer of hope. "I won't try to leave."

CHAPTER 4

James and Silk rode along the dirt-packed main street in Tucson. The community was bustling with activity now that the Civil War had ended and a large number of men were heading west to pursue new lives. The Arizona Territory was filled with army forts, and small communities were cropping up overnight. Some would prosper like Tucson, and others would become ghost towns. Saloons, mercantile stores, stables, a grocery store, and a whore house were in various stages of construction in Tucson.

James and Silk located the large railroad headquarters at the northern end of Tucson. The wood building stretched for half a block, and contained offices for engineers and accountants, a huge map room, meeting rooms, and suites for officers of the railroad when they came west to review progress on new construction. Building the new spur line from Tucson to Nogales had become a top priority, economically feasible because of the thousands of cattle being brought from the southern plains of the Arizona Territory and from Mexico to the many forts throughout the west and to California communities.

Victoria Barringer had been instrumental in persuading the railroad president, William Broadhurst, to convince stockholders that such an endeavor would be immediately lucrative. An extra incentive to Broadhurst had been to give him a portion of the cattle profits, a private agreement known only to Victoria Barringer and Broadhurst.

Barringer and Mathews tied their horses to the hitching rail and entered the building, noting several armed men stationed in different locations, plus men at the front and rear of the building.

A fat, baldheaded man looked up from the papers on the counter. "What da ya want?" he asked in a curt manner.

"Is Patch here?" Barringer asked.

"No one calls him by that name. His name is Larry, and he ain't here. What da ya want?" he said rudely.

Barringer leaned his elbows on the counter, his gaze never leaving the fat man's eyes. "No need to be nasty. I just wanted information on the time frame for construction of the spur line to Nogales."

Frank Bower suddenly seemed very uncomfortable being stared at by Barringer. Bower dropped his gaze to the papers in front of him. "You'll have to talk with O'Brien. He'll be back this afternoon." Two of the armed men moved towards the counter.

"Tell him that James Barringer stopped in. I'm a rancher who has cattle to move north, and I was wondering about the time frame for railroad construction," James said in a level voice. "A lot of us down near the border want to know." Barringer and Mathews turned and walked out of the building.

"Lots of men with guns," Silk noted. "He doesn't take any chances, and apparently he's got a lot of enemies."

"If he lives and works in that building, it will be difficult to get to him. But, I didn't smell any food. He probably eats in one of the restaurants or hotels," James guessed.

"Well, we can check out his movements. He's got to eat sometime," Silk noted.

"Let's go over to the Star Casino Hotel and see if Red Drago is in town," James stated.

The men walked to the hotel, a two-story building with a large white painted star encircled with the words Star Casino Hotel over the front entrance. The men entered the lobby and looked around. Several colored chairs and couches were scattered about the room, blue drapes hung on the sides of the windows, and large rugs in various Indian patterns were placed at different locations. Big pots with artificial flowers completed the rather nice surroundings. They walked up to the counter and were met by a young man in his early twenties with short, dark hair and smiling eyes.

"Can I help you?" he asked in a friendly tone of voice.

"We are looking for Red Drago," said Barringer.

The man's demeanor quickly changed, eyes becoming guarded and smile disappearing.

"He's in his room, but he's not to be disturbed."

James put his hands down hard on the counter. "He'll be disturbed today. I want you to tell us the room number, and then come out and sit down in one of these chairs," Barringer declared.

"I can't do that," he said in a fearful voice, eyes wide.

Silk Mathews cocked his repeating rifle and set it down sharply on the counter, pointing at the young man. "No need for you to be harmed in any way."

The clerk looked at the rifle and made a quick decision. "He's in Room 247 over the front of the building."

"What's your name?" Barringer asked.

"Mike…Mike Johnson."

"Come over here and sit down," said James, pointing to an overstuffed chair. The young man quickly obeyed.

James's eyes narrowed, his face hardened, anger and bitterness churning inside as he moved quickly up the stairs.

***

A minute earlier there had been a knock on Drago's door.

"Housekeeping!" said the young woman.

Drago was just waking up in the early afternoon after a night of gambling and drinking. He remembered that the woman was pretty with long dark pigtails, and watched her intently as she entered the room with cleaning supplies and a broom.

"What's your name?" Drago asked.

Suddenly seeming ill at ease, she replied, "Jackie…I can come back. I don't need to bother you now."

A sinister look caused his long face to take on the look of a killer rat as he moved towards the young woman.

She dropped her cleaning supplies. "No…please!" she cried out.

Drago grabbed her by the arm, threw her on the bed, and began tearing off her clothes. The young woman screamed as Drago pulled down his trousers and climbed on top of her. "Shut up and you won't get hurt," he growled. "I just want a little fun."

"No!" she cried out, and continued to fight.

***

James entered as the man and woman fought on the bed, grabbed the gunman by the arms, and tossed him like a rag doll to the other side of the room. With the quickness of a rodent, Drago was on his feet and grabbed his revolver from a holster hanging on a chair. James seized Drago's gun hand, smashed it against the wall, and the weapon went flying. Using his body as a battering ram, Drago hit Barringer in the stomach and then jumped forward to grab a knife off the bureau. The men circled each other warily.

"Who are you? Why are you after me?" he grunted.

Both men were breathing hard as they continued to circle one another.

"You killed a man and raped a woman on my ranch."

Drago had a quizzical look on his ugly face.

"They was just Mexicans."

"I'm a Mexican!" James said loudly, his eyes mirroring hatred.

Drago's eyes widened and he jumped forward, thrusting his knife at Barringer's stomach. James knocked the knife to one side, but not before it cut him along the right side. He grabbed Drago's hand and arm with both of his and yanked the arm down and across his knee. The bone snapped and Drago screamed in pain. Grabbing him by the throat, James backed Drago up to the window.

"You miserable bastard," Barringer growled. With a surge of strength, he hurled Drago through the second story window, taking out the window and the sash. Drago screamed as he plummeted downward, landing on his head, snapping his neck.

The loud crash through the window and Drago's shout made the young hotel clerk jump straight into the air as he saw the body fall into the street. "Oh, no!" he cried out. "Oh, no!"

Silk was out the front door in a flash, looked up, and saw James in the opening that had been the window. "Are you all right?" he yelled.

"I'm fine. Get the horses."

Mathews headed up the street on the run as James walked downstairs holding his bloody side. The hotel clerk was staring out the window at the dead man who was wearing no pants as townspeople began to gather.

"I need some bandages for a cut. Can you get some?" James asked.

"Yes," he said, and moved quickly to a back room to procure gauze and tape.

He returned a few moments later, bringing with him another of the hotel housekeepers, an older lady. "This woman is good at bandaging wounds," he said nervously, his gaze moving back and forth between James and the body in the street. The housekeeper stopped the bleeding and quickly put a bandage in place. Barringer grimaced in pain, but made no sound.

"You need to see a doctor about stitching up the wound," she stated. "This should hold until then." The housekeeper looked into James's eyes. "Thanks for helping Jackie. That Drago was an evil man, feared by all the hotel employees. Seeing him dead is like a dream come true."

"Thanks for bandaging me," he said, and gave her a quick smile.

***

Outside the hotel it was turning into a carnival atmosphere. The noisy crowd was milling around the half-naked body, talking in loud voices. James gave money to the hotel manager for the repair of the window and stepped outside. Everyone stared at the tall, powerfully built cowboy, and conversations momentarily quieted down.

***

Tucson Town Marshal Jasper Sullivan ran to the scene. A bystander talked with Sullivan, a man of medium height with close-cropped hair. He walked up to Barringer and glanced at his bloody shirt. "Do you want to tell me what happened?" Sullivan demanded.

Silk Mathews rode up with James's horse and sat quietly on his saddle, watching.

"Red Drago and Patch O'Brien killed a man on my ranch, raped his wife, then shot her and left her for dead, but she's still alive. I came after the two of them, fought with Drago in his room, and threw him out the window. Now I'm going after O'Brien. That's about the long and the short of it," James said in an angry voice.

"You can't take the law into your own hands around here. That's what the U. S. Marshal and the territorial judge are for," Sullivan said loudly. The town marshal glanced at the gathering crowd. "Someone get a blanket and cover the body," he yelled.

The crowd moved slowly towards the two men. "We really don't have time to argue with you," Silk interjected. Sullivan swung his head around and stared at Silk, whose rifle was cradled in his arm.

"Marshal, I'm James Barringer. You can send someone down south to our ranch. Victoria Barringer is my grandmother, and she'll verify who I am and what happened."

"You are going to have to come with me. Drago was killed in Tucson, which makes it my jurisdiction," said the steady if unspectacular lawman.

"You're not listening to me, and you don't seem to care about the victims on my ranch. What kind of a lawman are you?" James asked loudly.

Marshal Sullivan looked perplexed. "You can't talk to me like that. I'm the marshal!"

Barringer walked to his horse and mounted, a look of

anger on his face. "Don't get in my way," he growled.

Sullivan was brave, but had a wife and two small children and was not stupid. He quickly considered his options. "Tell you what. Stop at my office before you leave and fill out paperwork. I'll need to make a report for the town council," the marshal said loudly.

James wanted to help the lawman save face. "I'll make sure and do that, Marshal. I'll fill out whatever paperwork you need." The two cowboys turned their horses and rode away as the crowd began milling once again.

Sullivan felt confused, angry and relieved, all at the same time. "O'Brien doesn't know it yet, but he has a tiger looking for him," he said to himself.

CHAPTER 5

Larry O'Brien was angry. He returned to his headquarters to find that Barringer had killed his top gunman, and had actually entered his office to find him. His face was red, his mouth fixed in a snarl, and a large vein throbbed across his forehead as his good eye flashed from man to man in front of him. The men standing around had seen him mad before, but never this furious.

"Chuck," he bellowed. "Why didn't you send men after them when you learned about Drago's death?"

Chuck Davis, the assistant railroad superintendent, was frightened and perplexed as to how to answer that question. "I was waiting for you to return?" he sputtered.

The heavyset superintendent paced up and down, staring at the floor, and suddenly jerked his head up. "Did Tim Edwards get back with a rider named Bob Steele?" O'Brien roared.

"No sir. We haven't seen Edwards or Steele," Chuck noted.

O'Brien continued to pace. The men in front of him stood quietly. No one spoke. *I should have killed Edwards like Drago wanted*, O'Brien thought to himself. *What a mistake that was.*

"Send a rider down to Patagonia to find 'em and git 'em up here," said Larry.

"Yes sir," said Chuck as he left the room.

The front door opened, and all eyes were on Town Marshal Jasper Sullivan as he entered.

"Why the hell didn't you arrest them?" O'Brien blurted out.

Sullivan fixed him with a cold stare. "You and I need to talk in private."

"My office," O'Brien commanded, and walked into his office.

Sullivan followed him and closed the door. "Is what James Barringer said true?"

"Of course not," said O'Brien in a loud voice.

"He claims you shot a man on his ranch, raped his wife, and then shot her. She survived," the marshal stated.

"Survived? You mean she's alive?" Larry said in disbelief.

Sullivan suddenly knew the story was true, and Larry realized the blunder he had just made. O'Brien sat down heavily in his chair, and Sullivan took a seat across from the desk, intently watching O'Brien, who was staring at the ceiling. *If I kill Tim Edwards, then it will be her word against mine if this goes to court. Where the hell is Bob Steele?* he wondered.

"It's just her word against mine, and the railroad has high-priced lawyers. Right now, I'm going to surround myself with railroad men to protect myself from this crazy rancher," Patch noted.

"He's got another man with him, tall and blond-haired."

"So, there's two of 'em?"

Sullivan nodded.

"If you find out where they are, let me know," said O'Brien.

Sullivan stood up and walked from the office. Larry began to pace the floor, thinking of ways to draw Barringer out into the open.

***

During the next week, O'Brien was accompanied by eight railroad men wherever he went. At night, O'Brien had men stationed around and on top of the building. When he went to dinner, several men ate with him at the restaurant, and others surrounded the building. Twice he rode south to check out sites for the spur that needed additional engineering and cost estimates. His men spread out on both sides and in front when riding to and from the locations. One site in particular was difficult to gauge cost-wise, because the rails would have to go through or around a gorge between two low-lying mountainous areas. The added cost of making a half circle was being weighed against building the line through the gorge. O'Brien posted men on both sides of the gorge when he and his engineers and bodyguards traveled through.

***

Barringer and Mathews had been following his activities with great interest. They used binoculars to watch the railroad men's movements, always looking for a weak spot. James and Silk visited both summit locations and noted that the lookouts would always use the same two spots on either side of the deep, narrow pass. Cigarette butts were scattered around the two locations. As the railroad men started their return through the gorge, a shot would be fired and the two lookouts would stand up and wave their cowboy hats to signify that all was normal.

Sitting around their campfire at night, the two men began to formulate a plan. "First we need to overpower the lookouts. O'Brien is sending the same two men to the summit locations each time he goes through the pass. The men are comfortable with their job assignments and don't do anything but smoke and sleep," James pointed out.

"That appears to be the best spot to ambush them," Silk reasoned.

The following morning, just after sunrise, James and Silk hid their horses in a side canyon and climbed to the spots where the lookouts would be posted. The lookouts arrived at their spots just after nine o'clock and waved their hats to show that all was in order. Below, O'Brien and the party of railroad men made their way at a leisurely pace to the location where the surveyors and engineers were finishing their work. James signaled Silk, and the two men stepped out from their hiding place at the same time.

"Put your hands in the air and turn around," Barringer ordered.

The surprised lookout stared wide-eyed at James and raised his hands. "Don't shoot. I'm a married man," he blurted.

James tied him up and gagged him. The lookout was wearing a dark shirt as was Barringer, so James needed only to confiscate his dark hat for waving to the party below.

Silk Mathews was not as lucky with the other railroad man. Upon ordering him to raise his hands, the railroad employee moved partially behind a boulder and started to draw his weapon. Silk jumped forward and smashed his rifle barrel down on the man's head, knocking him to the ground before he could fire his weapon. After tying him up and gagging him, Mathews signaled that everything was ready.

They sat down, and the vigil began. Three hours later the party was ready to return through the gorge. A shot was fired and Barringer and Mathews both stood-up, waved their hats that belonged to the railroad men, and then sat back down.

When the slow-moving party of horsemen reached the spot below Silk and James, they were about thirty yards away.

Barringer stood up. "I want O'Brien. The rest of you can turn around and go," he yelled, his rifle pointed at the railroad superintendent.

"What the hell," O'Brien shouted.

Barringer fired a shot in front of the horses. The echo was loud, causing the horses to rear in the air.

"Shoot 'em," O'Brien commanded.

Most of the horses were rearing up in fear, bumping into animals next to them, and began whinnying loudly. One gunman had pulled his revolver and was trying to steady his horse so that he could get off an accurate shot. Silk shot him through the chest, and he fell backwards off the horse. The second rifle shot reverberated off the walls of the narrow canyon, creating more havoc among the horses, which were now whinnying and bucking, frantic to escape the narrow confines of the canyon.

A second gunman got a shot off in Silk's direction, but it was off the mark because his horse could not be controlled. Silk's second shot struck Bob Steele in the stomach, and he went down under the horses' hooves.

The melee was utter chaos below the Barringer duo. Horses were rearing and coming down on top of the horses next to them. The railroad men were holding on with both hands, trying not to be bucked off onto the ground where the horses' hoofs awaited them. No one but O'Brien even had a gun in his hand.

The railroad superintendent fired two wild shots at Barringer, but neither came close. Barringer took his time, aimed, and fired. The shot hit O'Brien in the right lung and his head jerked back, his one eye wide open as he yelled. O'Brien's horse reared into the air, tossing him over backwards. As he hit the ground, the horse behind him came downward and its hooves crushed O'Brien's skull.

Barringer and Mathews had their rifles up and ready to fire, but the railroaders' desire to do battle was gone. Slowly the railroad men got their horses under control and stared at the two men above them. Both of O'Brien's gunmen were dead, and there was no show of bravery.

"I'm not out to kill the rest of you," Barringer yelled out to the railroaders. "Unbuckle your gun belts and let them drop. Then, dismount."

The men did as they were ordered. James motioned for Silk to climb down, then Barringer descended. He had the railroad men tie the three bodies to their empty saddles. Only one of the men still had fight in him. A big, tall man with a red face and scraggly beard looked at Barringer with hatred in his eyes. "You killed my boss, and you're gonna' pay for it," he snarled.

James walked to him and smashed his revolver across the side of the man's head, knocking him to his hands and knees. His friends helped him mount his horse and he hung on to the saddle horn, eyes unable to focus.

"Listen up," James commanded. "My name is James Barringer. O'Brien and Drago killed a man on my ranch, raped and shot his wife, and left her for dead. Tell the marshal that I killed O'Brien. He knows where my ranch is located."

The expressions on the railroad workers' faces ranged from fear to disbelief.

"Mount up. My quarrel is not with you. Get going," James ordered, anger directed at everyone connected to O'Brien. The men rode up the canyon at a rapid pace. No one looked back. The cattlemen retraced their steps up to the summits, released the other two railroad employees, and sent them on their way.

CHAPTER 6

William Broadhurst, President of the Central Southern Railroad, had a scowl on his face as he exited the coach that had brought him from Tucson to the Barringer Ranch. Broadhurst was a distinguished looking and overweight executive who spent most of his life behind a desk in Chicago. He had curly salt and pepper hair, long sideburns that ended at his chin, a large expansive face, and heavy lips. His height helped him carry the extra poundage that pushed his weight to two hundred and sixty pounds. With him was Ronald Houston, U. S. Marshal in charge of The Arizona Territory. Houston was in his late fifties, had white hair, a thin face, piercing dark eyes, and carried his thin frame with a sense of purpose.

Victoria met them as they ascended her front porch stairs. Broadhurst introduced Houston in a polite but formal manner.

Houston's deep, resonating voice caused those around him to listen respectfully when he spoke. During his early days of chasing bad men, he developed a reputation for tenacity, and seldom missed apprehending the outlaws he was after. He was an intelligent, no-nonsense lawman who respected and upheld the laws of The United States of America.

The two men had decided to visit Victoria Barringer together. The killing in Tucson and the shootings outside of that city had made headlines throughout the southwest and also in Chicago, where the railroad had its central headquarters.

Members of the Board of Directors of the Central Southern Railroad had brought pressure to bear on the U. S. Marshal's office to determine immediately what the facts were. Why was a railroad superintendent killed, and was his reputation as disreputable as the newspapers suggested?

Broadhurst and Houston decided to go together to get all of the facts. The railroad president was in a secret business relationship with Victoria that he did not intend to disclose.

"I'm looking for your grandson, James Barringer," the marshal said in his deep voice.

"He's in Mexico right now. I have the victim of the rape and shooting here in my home. There was a witness to the crimes, and he's here," she said in a level voice. Her eyes never left the marshal's face.

"A witness!" Broadhurst said incredulously. "No one said anything about a witness." He took out a white handkerchief and wiped his forehead.

"He was riding with O'Brien and Drago. Apparently, his job was that of messenger for O'Brien," she explained. "He was not involved in what occurred."

"Let me get this straight," said Houston. "He was riding with those two but wasn't involved? That sounds strange."

"He's just a boy of seventeen. He said they would have killed him if he had intervened. Carmen Rodriguez, the young woman who was raped and shot, corroborated his story."

"If you will take me to them, I'll interview them now," Houston stated gruffly, with no semblance of politeness.

"Maria," Victoria called out.

A fat woman, whose age was difficult to detect, appeared and led the marshal into the ranch house. Victoria and Broadhurst followed, but went into her office and sat down.

"You have no idea what serious pressure I'm under," he blurted out. "The board of directors wants prosecution of those involved in O'Brien's death. He was a good employee for years."

"He was a murderer and a rapist. The trail of your railroad line is littered with the buried bodies of Irish, German, and Chinese who he killed for objecting to his brutish methods. If newspaper reporters begin questioning railroad employees, the truth will come out."

Broadhurst let out a groan and wiped his face again with his handkerchief.

Victoria continued. "The two men who were shot in the gorge were hired gunmen. One, named Bob Steele, was wanted for murder in the New Mexico Territory. I do my homework."

"Oh, God," the railroad president exclaimed. "I knew he was tough on the workers, but he always made the deadlines for construction. And that, in the railroad business, is the bottom line."

"You are just going to have to bite the bullet and tell the board of directors the truth. Here's my recommendation... indicate that he was a good employee who always finished the jobs on time. Tell them he worked for the railroad for a number of years and was tough, but had never been accused of serious crimes. This time, he crossed the line and was guilty of rape and murder. Had the facts reached you, you would have dismissed him and helped in the prosecution of both men. Emphasize that you would have done the right thing. It's important that they believe you."

Broadhurst was sweating profusely, continually wiping

his face with a handkerchief. "You're right, I suppose. That's about the best defense I can think of."

Victoria's eyes narrowed and she fixed the railroad president with a hard stare. "Do you think this will affect bringing the spur line down to Nogales as we planned?"

Broadhurst thought for a moment. "I don't think so. The numbers involving the movement of cattle across the border are there to make it work. The bottom line is what concerns the board members."

"Good. Then we'll go forward as planned," she stated. "I'm buying a ranch on the other side of the border to use as a staging area for cattle herds. It should make it easier for my family and for the Mexican dons who gather cattle for marketing."

Broadhurst wiped the sweat off his face again. He brightened up at the thought of additional money for himself from the proceeds of the contract with Victoria. "How much...?"

"Your share should about equal your income as a railroad president," Victoria emphasized. "Keep the program moving forward."

"Oh, I will," he emphasized.

They were interrupted by a knock on the door.

"Come in," she said.

U. S. Marshal Ronald Houston entered the room and sat down with them. He had notes taken during the interviews with Carmen Rodriguez and Tim Edwards.

"Well, the facts of the case are pretty clear. The rape and murder did take place, according to the witnesses. The kid was too afraid to do anything, and he didn't realize that they would try to kill her before they left. No jury would convict your grandson of crimes involving the deaths of Larry O'Brien and Red Drago, even though he did murder them.

"Now, regarding the two dead men," Houston continued. "Bob Steele was wanted for murder, so it's doubtful that James Barringer would be found guilty of any charge involving Steele. That leaves the last gunman, a man named Lou Neeley. It seems I remember a warrant being issued for him some time ago, but I don't remember what it was for. I'll check when I get back to the office."

Both Victoria and William Broadhurst were listening attentively.

"I'll need James Barringer to come to my office in Lordsburg, New Mexico, and make written statements about what occurred. Right now, there won't be a warrant issued for his arrest," Houston stated.

Broadhurst looked relieved. "You mean you aren't going to bring any charges against Barringer?"

"I couldn't convict him of anything right now. I don't waste time arresting someone and trying them in court when I can't get a conviction. I have many more crimes to investigate and an extreme shortage of time," the marshal explained. "Mrs. Barringer, if I can buy a horse, I'd appreciate it. I'm not going back with Bill. I'm heading over to Sierra Vista to investigate the killing of a silver miner. The U. S. government will send you thirty dollars for the horse and saddle."

Victoria's eyes sparkled. "Yes. That can be arranged."

The three people concluded their business over lunch and then moved to the front porch of the ranch house as a cowhand brought a horse for Houston. The marshal's eyes widened as he stared at the magnificent black stallion that stood in front of them.

"Why, I can't take...." Houston complained without much conviction.

"Nonsense. As long as I get the thirty dollars from the federal government, the horse is yours," she replied.

The marshal walked around the animal, running his hand along its side. "This is one of the most beautiful stallions I've ever seen," Houston stated. "There's the matter of the saddle. This one is far too expensive."

"Consider it a part of the sale of the horse," she said in a friendly voice, smiling.

The marshal mounted the horse and rode it in a small circle. He was lost in thought as he pulled up in front of Victoria.

"I appreciate the lunch," said the grinning marshal. "You make sure you have James come and see me when he has time."

They said their goodbyes, and the marshal rode away at a gallop, testing the response and stride of the stallion. The taciturn lawman had a smile on his face, highly unusual for him.

CHAPTER 7

At the same time the meeting was transpiring on the Barringer Ranch, James Barringer was crossing the international border with Mexico. He rode up to a small community named The Crossing and dismounted in front of a stable that included stalls, a tack room, an office, and an adjoining barn. Barringer patted his favorite palomino, Oro, and walked into the small office, a wide grin on his face.

Paco Flores's face lit up at the sight of James Barringer, who was about to become Ricardo Montoya.

"Chameleon! I had a feeling you would be along soon."

Flores kept a change of clothes for James, and the tall cowboy changed from Arizona cowboy clothes to Mexican clothing when he crossed the border. The reverse was true when he returned to the Arizona Territory.

"It's good to see you, my friend," he told Flores as the men shook hands.

Flores was short, heavy-set, and had a face that looked like Santa Claus. His white hair framed a wide face, large dark eyes, and a smiling mouth. Paco's white beard was close cropped, and around the eyes he had friendly wrinkles from smiling.

"Is someone chasing you again? Is that why you're here?" he responded, a twinkle in his eyes.

"No. This time I'm on a business trip. In fact, I would like your advice. But, let me change clothes first."

Flores pointed to a small adjoining room. Montoya walked in, opened a closet door, and took out his favorite beige leather outfit. He put on a white shirt with a white silk scarf around the neck. Next, he got into tight fitting leather pants with shiny metal loops up and down the sides of the legs, held in place by silver buttons. He slipped on a very short matching jacket with heavy embroidery and silver buttons. Lastly, he added a sombrero with a great deal of silver embroidery around the brim.

"Such a regal look! You are every inch the don," Flores said, and grinned. "Don Diego Salazar must have been jealous when you two were together. You look more like a don than he did."

Ricardo thought for a moment. *That might have been part of the problem at the end of our relationship.* Montoya remembered that Don Diego must have seen his abilities at an early age, and saw to it that he was well educated, became fluent in English, and well trained with a revolver and rifle. Ricardo quickly ascended to the role of segundo, or second in command, and began handling all of the don's business ventures across the border. Don Diego hated gringos, and let Ricardo oversee moving herds into Arizona that brought the don hundreds of thousands of dollars.

"He wasn't always as mean and devious as he was towards the end of his life. He was a shrewd businessman in the early years and would listen to reason. It wasn't until he sustained head injuries from a horse throwing him into boulders that he started to change. I think he was in pain much of the time."

Paco seldom said anything negative about people. "I only knew him as an angry, nasty person. I don't mean to say bad things, but he was a mean man."

The two men walked up to a small cantina, sat outside in the cool afternoon, and ordered soup and enchiladas. Ricardo sighed. "I miss the food, the beer, and the informal lifestyle. It was a good life," he reminisced. They chatted for a few minutes, and the conversation came back to Ricardo's days as segundo on El Rancho Grande, where he thought he had been born.

"As I was saying, it wasn't until the horse threw him and he fractured his skull that Don Diego began to change. A lot of clear brain liquid escaped from his head, and the terrible headaches began. It just changed him entirely."

"What caused him to try and kill you?"

Ricardo shook his head in disgust. "I refused an order to have Apache women and children murdered. I refused in front of the vaqueros, and it was a great embarrassment to Don Diego. He lost face, and I lost my job. He sent me back to the hacienda and then sent a man to kill me. I killed the assassin and was forced to run."

The men finished their beers, replaced immediately by two more cold ones. Two vaqueros walked up to the cantina. Both looked at Ricardo with skepticism and dislike. They placed an order for food to be delivered up the street to their father's home and slowly walked away, still giving Ricardo nasty looks.

"They are the Baca twins. They aren't very friendly, but their father usually keeps them under control," said Paco. He grinned at Montoya. "They don't like your clothes. Too upper class for this village."

"You know why I change clothes, don't you?"

"Sure. You get respect from men if you look like them."

"That, and it's difficult to give orders to men if you don't wear clothing similar to theirs," Ricardo stated. "They resent it."

"And you are always giving orders," Paco said and laughed, as did Ricardo.

"I need your advice. My grandmother, Victoria Barringer, wants to purchase the ranch owned by Don Jorge Franco near the mountains east of here. What is your opinion of that property?"

Paco Flores whistled. "That would be a difficult place in which to live and work. An Apache chief named Sky Walker and his band live in that mountain range. Don Jorge tried on several occasions to drive them out, but he couldn't do it. The last time, his son was badly wounded. He's given up and gone back to Mexico City, where his family has holdings."

Montoya nodded his head in understanding. "I've had a few run-ins with Sky Walker over the years. He's a determined man, and wants his people to live free."

Flores fixed Montoya with a knowing gaze. "Don't we all want to live free?"

"Do the raiding parties come from Sky Walker's band?"

Paco thought for a moment.

"I don't think so. His people live in those meadows up in the mountains. They grow crops and just want to be left alone, or so I'm told."

"Where do you get this information?"

"There's a half Apache woman named Chata who lived with her Mexican husband on the ranch. I don't know if they are still there. But, she seems to know a lot about Sky Walker. I think she has relatives in the band."

"That's my next stop, then. I'll see if I can locate her at the rancho."

The white-bearded man seemed dismayed. "What good will that do?"

"I would like to meet with Sky Walker and determine if we could work out an arrangement."

Paco shook his head slowly from side to side. "You can't make friends with the Apaches."

"I'm not talking about friendship. But a truce might be an idea. They are men, just like the two of us, and want the same things…to live and be free."

The two friends chatted for some time. Paco sent a messenger to the ranch to determine if anyone was still living there, and he returned just before dark. "Chata and her husband are still there. She doesn't like living in the mountains," said the messenger, Jose Gutierrez. "I told her you would come tomorrow."

Early the next morning Ricardo set out on the ten-mile ride towards the hacienda owned by Don Jorge Franco, traveling through grass two to three feet high in many spots, cattle dotting the golden grasslands. Gradually Montoya began the ascent to higher ground as small mountains came into view. In the distance he spotted the tall main adobe building, an L-shaped structure with a courtyard in the center and two-foot thick outer walls encircling the courtyard. Around the top of the building on the interior was a walkway to be used by riflemen to fire down on Apaches or banditos. A kitchen, large living room, dining room, and five bedrooms were built along the inside walls. The home looked like a white fortress with one large entrance gate. Scattered in many locations around the main hacienda were small adobe huts that the peons had lived in when Don Jorge's rancho was a thriving cattle ranch.

Montoya dismounted and walked his palomino through the main gate. Chata, a thin woman of Mexican and Apache ancestry, walked towards him while wiping her hands on her apron. Ricardo could smell food being cooked.

"Good morning, Chata. My name is Ricardo Montoya."

"Paco's messenger said you would come," she stated as her eyes moved quickly over the tall Mexican standing in front of her. "You are the one who hunts Apaches."

"I used to before I knew better. I don't anymore. My family wants to buy this hacienda from Don Jorge. We would build it into a large cattle ranch again. You and your husband would be welcome to stay."

"Come into the kitchen and eat," she said in a noncommittal voice.

Ricardo followed her into the building and introduced himself to her husband, Manuel, a hugely fat Mexican whose jowls hung several inches below his chin. Manuel loved to eat, drink beer, and sleep, and it showed.

The food was excellent, and Montoya complimented Chata on her cooking.

"I would like to meet with Sky Walker."

"He knows of you and what you have done," she noted.

"What do you mean?"

"I was with Sky Walker's people when you and the Russian general attacked and killed most of his band. He remembers you."

Ricardo studied her for a moment. He realized she probably was living at the rancho to gather information for Sky Walker and to alert him if trouble was imminent. Manuel was her excuse for being there.

Montoya and a group of vaqueros, together with General Constantine Vorshoff and his troops, had cornered Sky

Walker's band in the mountains and killed more than three quarters of the Apaches. Vorshoff had been a Russian army officer who joined the Mexican army and was promoted to the rank of general. He was given Mexican citizenship and two large land holdings in return for leading the fight against the Apaches in northern Mexico. Vorshoff had been very successful, and his reputation continued to grow.

"You were one of those who survived?" Ricardo asked.

Chata looked at Ricardo with guarded interest. "My mother's sister and her son were both killed there."

"We cannot change history. But we can try to change our actions towards one another. Tell him I no longer hunt Apaches," Montoya said in an even voice.

"I will tell him. I should be back by dark," she noted.

The half Apache, half Mexican woman walked quickly into the foothills and disappeared. Her husband snored loudly from an enormous chair on the veranda. Ricardo wandered about the hacienda, thinking it was more like a fort than a home. *But, if peace ever comes, it could be torn down and rebuilt into a beautiful hacienda*, he reasoned.

Chata returned just before dark. Her husband was hungry and let her know it, sounding as if he hadn't eaten for a week. She ignored him and walked over to Ricardo.

"He will see you tomorrow. Just follow the trail into the mountains."

"Where should I go to find him?"

"He will find you."

Montoya headed into the mountain foothills the following morning and began the upward ascent. The trail made a number of switchbacks as the elevation increased. Soldiers could be ambushed in a dozen spots, making it nearly impossible for troopers to mount an assault. It was a relatively safe place in which to live, he reasoned. Rounding the corner of a large rock formation, Ricardo came face to face with the Indian chief astride a large chestnut stallion.

***

Sky Walker was a big man with broad shoulders, a granite-like body, and huge legs. His head was large and featured a prominent nose, square jaw, and enormous dark eyes. The buckskin clad chief wore his hair shoulder length, held in place by a dark red bandanna tied behind his head. His trousers and vest were covered in beaded patterns. Sky Walker wore no shirt under the vest, thereby accenting his biceps. He nodded at Montoya, and Ricardo responded in like fashion.

"Thank you for meeting with me. Can we dismount and talk?" Ricardo asked in Spanish.

"Follow me," Sky Walker replied in a deep voice. He turned his horse around on the trail and they went upward for another seventy-five yards before entering a small clearing. Both men dismounted and sat on flat boulders that were placed at numerous locations. Montoya realized this was a meeting place where ceremonies probably were conducted.

"Why are you here?" Sky Walker asked in perfect Spanish.

"My family wants to buy the rancho just below us. I have no quarrel with the Apaches and want to live in peace."

"There is no peace between our peoples."

"There could be if men on both sides made an attempt," Ricardo stated.

Sky Walker's large penetrating eyes bore into Montoya. Ricardo returned the stare with the same even look.

"Why are you buying this rancho?" the chief asked. "I heard you were living in the Arizona Territory."

"I was born in Arizona. My family there wants to expand

their cattle operations, and this rancho would be a central location for holding cattle before herding them into Arizona."

Sky Walker seemed confused but curious. "We clashed in Arizona when you were dressed in cowboy clothing, and in Mexico when you wore the clothes you have on today. The only thing that is the same is your palomino."

"That is true," said Ricardo. He explained about being raised on the Salazar Rancho, finding out when his Mexican father was dying that he actually was born in the Arizona Territory, and discovering his Barringer heritage.

"Where have you chosen to live?" Sky Walker asked.

"It is not my choice. I fell out of favor with Don Diego Salazar, and later he put a price on my head. I feel more comfortable in Mexico, in these clothes with these people, but my future is in the Arizona Territory. Often we don't get to choose, life does it for us."

Sky Walker studied Montoya as he spoke and concluded that Ricardo was honest in his explanation. "I would rather be living free in the Arizona Territory, but never on a reservation. Our people are treated like cattle on reservations, so we live here. We live free and enjoy our lives, although we would prefer to be somewhere else."

Ricardo smiled and nodded his head in understanding. The two men realized that events, plus fate, had channeled their lives down roads that they had not voluntarily chosen. Sky Walker returned his attention to the present. "Why would it be of benefit to me and my band to agree to such a thing?"

"The men at the ranch below would not be allowed to come into the mountains. You would be able to live in peace," Montoya explained.

"I drove the men away that lived below. Now it is peaceful," the chief pointed out.

Ricardo could tell that Sky Walker was interested, because the chief continued to engage him in conversation.

"More men will return, and in greater numbers. The Mexican army, in time, will come to drive you out. The Mexicans will demand it."

Sky Walker stood up, stretched, and looked out at the golden grasslands below. "Why should I trust you? You have killed many of my people," he pointed out as he studied Ricardo.

Montoya stood up and walked over to the chief. "You have killed many of my people, including Don Diego Salazar at our last encounter. One of your people drove a spear through his stomach."

The Indian chief grunted in remembrance. "Was he dressed in black clothing?"

Ricardo looked surprised. "Yes. He always dressed in black."

"Then I killed him. I remember the look on his face when I put the spear through him."

Montoya didn't know what to say for a few moments. "He didn't have many friends," Ricardo observed.

Sky Walker studied Montoya. He liked what he saw, reasoning that Ricardo was a strong leader among his people, appeared to be honest, and was straight forward in his speech. *He is not deceitful*, the chief thought.

"If we agree to a truce, it would be limited," said the Apache chief.

"Limited how?"

"It would apply only to your ranch. My people live here in freedom, and raiding bands do not stay here. I'm not against raiding, but I don't want the Mexican army following them back to where we now live. More women and children would die." Montoya nodded his head in understanding.

"When the raiding parties come here to visit their relatives, I will tell them that your ranch can not be raided. It's doubtful that they would refuse to follow my wishes, because I would not let them return here to visit their relatives if they lie to me," the chief noted.

"I understand," said Ricardo. "None of my men will enter the mountains, and they will not attack your braves if they are seen in the foothills. Also, you can have all of the beef that you need for your people," Ricardo said. "I'll drive a small herd up into the foothills."

Both men were quiet, lost in their own thoughts.

"It's a strange world where men hunt and kill each other like animals," Ricardo said in a bemused tone of voice.

The two men's eyes met and held.

"You have changed since the days when you led your vaqueros against us time after time."

"It never solved anything," Montoya said quietly.

Three Apaches came down the trail and into the clearing. Their leader jumped off his horse and ran over to the chief. Red Lance was of the same build as his father, Sky Walker.

"Kill him, Father! We should not be seen meeting with the enemy!" he shouted. The young Apache was dressed in a loin cloth and leggings, had red paint on his face, and his upper torso was bare. Red Lance had a knife in a sheath at his side and carried a newer repeating rifle.

"Stay where you are. I invited this man, Ricardo Montoya, to meet with me. This is none of your concern," Sky Walker commanded.

"To meet with the enemy is wrong! Why are you doing this?" Red Lance asked.

"Montoya is buying the ranch below the mountains. He

has agreed that his vaqueros will not kill Apaches. We can live in peace here. In return, we will not raid or harm the men and women on his ranch. I have given my word."

As Red Lance swung his rifle upward, Sky Walker reached out, grabbed the barrel, and pulled it from his son's grasp. Ricardo glanced over at his horse where his holster and revolver were hooked over the saddle horn. The other two braves moved forward.

"Would you dishonor your father?" Sky Walker said sharply.

The chief's attention turned to the other two braves, whom he had never seen before. Sky Walker cocked the rifle. "Stand back!" he told them.

The braves stopped moving forward.

"The three of you go up to the camp and wait for me. I will be there shortly. Go!" he ordered.

Red Lance's eyes were mere slits, and his teeth were clenched together in anger. He hesitated, then turned and mounted his horse. The other braves followed his lead and the trio slowly climbed the trail.

Sky Walker's gaze followed his son as he moved out of sight. "I have not seen him for some time. He has two men with him, probably from the Arizona reservations, and he will try to convince men from my band to join him. Red Lance is an angry young man who hates the reservation where braves are treated like dogs. He has been free most of his life, and believes it is a warrior's duty to raid, loot, and kill."

"Not having freedom is a terrible thing," Ricardo acknowledged. "In my case, it's not knowing what country I belong in. I feel that I am a Mexican, but the longer I live in the Arizona Territory the more at ease I become in body and mind. It is...a strange feeling."

Sky Walker had never had a long conversation with a Mexican or United States citizen. The only conversations he had had were with Indian agents on the reservation, and none of them were pleasant. Montoya's background story was intriguing to him. "I have killed many white men, and you have killed many Apaches. What did we accomplish? Nothing," the chief said in a deep voice. "Now my son is starting down the same path." He looked up the trail. "I must go now."

"I will keep my end of the agreement," Ricardo stated.

"And I will from my side. My people need to know that no one is going to come up the mountain to kill them."

Montoya mounted his horse, buckled on his revolver, and raised his hand in salute to Sky Walker. The chief did the same.

Fifteen minutes later, Sky Walker had reached one of the Indian camps spread throughout the lower mountain meadows. Hogans were all around the meadow composed of earthen walls supported by timbers, and most had campfire locations near them. More than two dozen hogans lined the meadow. His band had grown from about twenty to more than one hundred Apaches. Women were busy cooking while young children romped around the meadow. The braves in the band stood silently watching their leader as Sky Walker motioned for his son to join him and entered his hogan.

"Sit and let us talk," said the chief. "I have not seen you for months. Where have you been?"

"Deep in Mexico. The raiding was good until the Mexican army came after us. They caught us at night and killed all but the three of us. We need to rest and then begin raiding again. We killed many Mexicans."

"What did it accomplish?"

"We live like men, taking what we want when we feel like

it. It's the way of the warrior."

"And now there are only three of you left."

Red Lance gazed steadily at his father. "I will live free until I die."

"The people here live free. But these men have wives and children and will continue to provide for their families. No one will be permitted to live here and conduct raids."

"That's craziness!" his son declared. "We were born to raid and kill."

"You and your men do not have families. You think differently when you have a family."

"Father, you have grown old."

"I pray to the spirits of our ancestors. Continuing to war on the Mexicans is not the path to a successful life. The path of life is to live harmoniously with others."

Red Lance got to his feet. "There are three men here who want to join us.

Will you try to stop them?"

"No. But I will send their families back to the reservation. And they cannot return here. And you cannot return here again."

A shocked expression spread across Red Lance's face, and his mouth opened slightly. "You would turn away your own son?" he barked angrily.

"Yes. I will honor the agreement I have with the ranch people below this mountain. We will not fight them, and they will let us live in peace."

"I honor no such agreement!" the son yelled as he got up and left.

Sky Walker emerged from the hogan and walked over to where the other two members of the raiding party were talking to several men from his band.

"Hear me," said the chief. "I have an agreement with the Mexicans on the ranch below us. We will not raid the ranch, and they will not hunt us. From this day forward, any man joining a raiding party will no longer be welcome here. And his family will be sent back to the reservation."

The men began talking excitedly among themselves. After a few minutes, it was decided that they would not join Red Lance's band. The chief's son walked over to his father, furious at being embarrassed.

"I no longer respect you as a chief," he snarled. "I will continue to conduct war on Mexicans and those Anglos in the United States. And I will hunt down and kill the one you call Ricardo Montoya."

He and his two followers renewed their supplies and departed. Sky Walker felt a great sadness, for he loved his son and was proud of him and the status he had achieved. But he feared this would be the last time he would see him alive.

CHAPTER 8

Ricardo Montoya let Oro graze on the fertile grass atop a small hill while he stared out at El Rancho Grande, the huge Mexican ranch that spilled downward from its hilltop headquarters, a gigantic white home. Surrounding hills and valleys were strewn with smaller white adobe houses where the peons and vaqueros lived. The landscape was covered with patches of green, brown, and black, depending on the season and what crops were being grown. Gold grasslands shimmered in the sunlight around the perimeter of what had become a small town. Montoya had been in charge of erecting buildings, clearing and leveling land for new construction of adobe homes, widening the roads leading into the complex, and constructing outbuildings and corrals.

Two trails led upward to the imposing two-story house. Don Diego Salazar had installed a beautiful wrought iron balcony around the second level which housed his living quarters so he could leisurely survey his holdings. A feeling of openness and freedom was mingled with security against Apache raids.

Ricardo mounted Oro and began the ride into the valleys

leading to the rancho. He exchanged greetings with numerous vaqueros, who took off their sombreros in honor of their former segundo as he rode by. He passed farming fields, corrals, groves of fruit and nut trees, and dozens of small adobe houses. Ricardo smiled and waved to many of the families he had known for years, and who held him in high esteem for his fair and honest dealings. This show of reverence by the common people made Ricardo feel humble, and thankful to have played a role in so many peons' lives.

Don Diego had stripped Ricardo of his rank after he refused to kill Apache women and children, and twice sent assassins to kill him. Salazar later was killed by the Indians during a raid on Sky Walker's camp deep within Mexico. The don's son, Francisco, now ruled at El Rancho Grande.

Ricardo dismounted at the entrance to the fortress-like home. His brother, Rafael, walked down the front stairs and the two men embraced and talked for several minutes. They looked a great deal alike, although Rafael was half a head shorter. Both were well-built, had large heads, strong noses, broad chins, and curly black hair. Rafael sported a moustache and close-cropped goatee, while Ricardo was clean shaven.

"Brother. It took you a long time to get here," said a smiling Rafael.

"It's a long story. I'll tell you when we can talk privately."

"Let's go and meet with Francisco," Rafael suggested.

"What's it been like to work for him?' Ricardo asked.

"It's been good, and it was easy to make the move from head of his bodyguards to segundo. He takes great interest in the running of the rancho, and solicits my advice before he makes important decisions. He's really been quite easy to work for," Rafael said in a low voice.

"Then are you sure you want to leave?

"Quite sure. I want to be an owner and a don, not a manager all my life."

Ricardo laughed. "What did you tell Francisco about our trip to Hermosillo?"

"I told him we wanted a little vacation together to make new friends among the senoritas. He understood."

Ricardo grinned. "I'm ready for good food, wine, and senoritas, not necessarily in that order."

They entered the home, walked upstairs to Francisco's private quarters, and were shown to his office. Francisco came forward, and the two men shook hands.

"You've not changed any. You still look like you own your own rancho," he said, referring to Ricardo's expensive, beige colored clothing.

"Well you have changed, Francisco. Your clothing is very impressive."

Don Francisco Salazar was dressed in light blue tight fitting slacks, a matching jacket, and a white silk shirt. The outfit was covered with embroidery, and gold buttons ran down the sides of his pants and the front of his jacket.

"I don't like the dark colors that my father used to wear. When he died, I burned them all," said Francisco. "It's best to let go of the past and move forward."

Ricardo nodded his head in agreement and smiled.

There was no malice in the young don's voice. Rafael had assured Ricardo that Francisco held no grudge because of his father's death, related to an ill-fated attempt to capture or kill Montoya.

"I've even made friends with Don Carlos Bustamante, and we have no quarrel anymore. In fact, I wanted to call on his daughter, but found out she is engaged to a man in Mexico City," said Salazar.

Ricardo wondered if Francisco knew the background involving his failure to marry Maria Bustamante. The three men chatted for near thirty minutes before Salazar stood up, signaling the end of the meeting.

"If I don't see you before we leave in the morning, I want to wish you the best," said Ricardo.

Salazar smiled. "I know you will be forever linked with this rancho. You will always be welcome here."

"Thank you," Ricardo replied. "I appreciate your hospitality."

Early the next morning, the two brothers set out on the two day trip southward to Hermosillo. Again the vaqueros and peons took off their hats out of respect for Ricardo and Rafael as they passed by. During the ride, Ricardo told his brother about the rape and murder on the Barringer Ranch, and his successful search for the criminals.

"This man, O'Brien, was the superintendent of the railroad. Won't that create problems with the authorities?" Rafael asked.

"Probably, but I leave that to my grandmother. She has a remarkable ability to work with people and achieve her goals."

"I'm surprised that she would give me half ownership in Don Jorge Franco's rancho without ever having met me. She must trust you and your recommendations without reservation."

"She does. She watched me take over management of the Barringer Ranch and run it in the same way I did El Rancho Grande. The fact that you have taken my place and have done an equally good job speaks for your competence. She trusts my recommendations."

"I have not seen this rancho we are about to purchase,"

Rafael noted. "Is there much work to be done?"

Ricardo looked at his brother and smiled. "Everything."

The two men laughed. Ricardo told Rafael about his meeting with Apache Chief Sky Walker and the agreement they reached.

"Can you trust him?"

"He's an honorable man. He has killed many Mexicans and Anglos, but he is older and wiser now and wants to live in peace. He also wants his freedom, and can't have it on a reservation."

"So, our men are not to go into the mountains, and his braves will not raid our hacienda?"

"That's the plan." said Ricardo in a somewhat skeptical voice.

"You don't sound totally convinced," Rafael observed.

"Sky Walker will keep his word. It's his son I'm concerned about. Red Lance is a hot headed young brave with hatred in his heart. He won't have many followers, but they will be dedicated raiders. So, as you begin rebuilding the ranch, your men must be careful."

Rafael nodded his head in understanding. "We should be able to get vaqueros and peons in Hermosillo to start with. Offer a little money and they will come running. Also, once we've rebuilt the ranch, there are several experienced vaqueros who will follow me from the Salazar hacienda."

"Be careful," Ricardo warned. "We don't want to begin another blood feud with a Salazar. If you take too many of his top men it could create a real problem. We have a large Mexican population on the Barringer Ranch. I know of several good men you can talk with about joining you in Mexico."

"I'm anxious to see the rancho," Rafael responded.

"I visited Father and Mother's grave sites before I went

to the Salazar rancho. We had such great times. Family meant everything to them. I hope someday to have a family like that," Ricardo said.

"You sound like you are in a marrying mood," Rafael commented.

"After what happened with Maria Bustamante, I don't think so." His mind returned to the meeting he had had with Maria in the living room of her father's home.

***

"Maria, you don't seem pleased to see me," he had said.

"I'm pleased to see that you are still alive, Ricardo."

"I don't understand."

"I think you do," she said emphatically. "You have been involved in one shooting incident after another for as long as I have known you. You've been shot more than once and so far, survived. How long do you think you can continue to live this way and stay alive?"

Her beautiful dark eyes stared at him from a lovely, light-complexioned face surrounded by long, dark hair. She was a beautiful young woman who knew her own mind.

"These are violent times in northern Mexico," he said quietly. "There isn't much law enforcement. A man has to do what he thinks is right."

"That's part of your problem. You are not a judge and jury, but you act like you are," she said in an accusatory tone of voice.

Ricardo could not believe what he was hearing. One of the persons he had saved was her father, Don Carlos Bustamante, and Ricardo was shot while doing so.

"I do what I think is right. Many men don't or can't," he explained.

"Oh, Ricardo," she said, and dropped her gaze to the floor.

"If you keep on like this, always fighting for what you think is right, you won't live long."

Ricardo knew the conversation was going badly. "I love you, Maria, and I want to marry you."

Maria looked him squarely in the eyes. "I love you, too. But, I won't marry you. I want a husband who will be alive to watch his sons and daughters grow up. You are not that man. You have some deep fixation about justice at all costs. It will kill you," Maria exclaimed.

"I can try to change," he said softly, hardly believing he had uttered those words. But he loved her and wanted to marry her, even if it meant changing his lifestyle and altering his methods.

Maria was shaking slightly and close to tears. "I'm sorry, Ricardo. I don't think you can change." Ricardo stepped forward to take her in his arms, but she pushed him away. "I'm leaving for Mexico City next week. Juan Dominguez has asked me to marry him, and I said yes."

Montoya took a step backwards and looked at Maria as if she had betrayed him. The Dominguez family had food processing plants and stores throughout the Mexico City area, and had become a very wealthy family. Juan was first born and therefore the heir to the food empire.

Through sheer will power and the strength of his convictions, Ricardo had overcome nearly every obstacle that had appeared before him. Now he felt defeated, a feeling that was foreign to him.

"I'd like you to think this over."

"I've thought about this every day since you left. I'm going to marry Juan," she replied in a determined voice. Their eyes locked, and he could see there was no changing her mind. He turned and walked from the room, thinking he would never see Maria again.

***

Ricardo's mind returned to the present and he looked over at his brother. "I forgot to ask you, what happened to your engagement?"

Rafael looked chagrined. "Oh. It was embarrassing. The closer it got to the wedding day, the more I started to feel trapped. Finally, I just broke it off. She created a terrible scene. Her father wanted to shoot me. Her mother wanted to stick a knife in me. Her relatives, of which there were dozens, wanted to burn me at the stake."

Ricardo began laughing.

"It's no laughing matter. They made life miserable for me for weeks. Finally, she married a vaquero and things quieted down. But every time I see her coming, I turn around and go in the opposite direction. She still has that killing look in her eyes."

Ricardo was laughing almost hysterically. "That's the best laugh I've had in months."

Rafael threw a sheepish look at his brother. "Even the priest said I should look for another church to attend. But there's only one church on the ranch. Wow, were those people mad."

All Ricardo could do was wipe his eyes with his sleeve, because he was laughing so hard. "When the priest wants to cut your balls off, you know you're in trouble."

Oro, Ricardo's palomino, reared with concern over the noise his owner was making.

CHAPTER 9

Hermosillo was a bustling, mid-sized city in northwestern Mexico, the main economic center for the State of Sonora, with ranching, farming, and a small amount of manufacturing being the main sources of income. The two brothers rode up the main street and stopped at a bank, and then continued on to the law office of Alfredo Garcia, purported to be one of the most reputable lawyers in that city. The exterior of the building was painted light brown and had two large windows in front. An overhang was built over the wooden sidewalk to afford shade for clients and passersby.

They entered the large law office and saw a number of clerks and young women sitting at desks writing legal documents for their employer. One of the female employees went to Garcia's private office and informed him that he had visitors, and the influential attorney walked up to the front to greet the Montoya brothers.

Garcia was a tall man in his mid-forties with long side burns, a broad forehead, large nose, and friendly eyes. He wore a starched white shirt and a small black tie to match his suit. Shiny black shoes completed the ensemble.

The Montoya brothers introduced themselves and Garcia led them back to his plush, beautifully appointed office. The walls were lined with shiny oak, and the chairs were covered with soft calve's skin. His desk was mahogany, and beautiful paintings adorned the walls. Garcia's office conveyed the impression of dignity and success. They exchanged pleasantries for a few minutes and then got down to business.

"I deposited the down payment money in the Hermosillo Bank before we came here," Ricardo noted.

"Good. I will begin drawing up the purchase contract for the rancho owned by Don Jorge Franco. I have his power of attorney to close the sale once Victoria Barringer reads and signs the contract and returns it to me, along with the remaining monies. Everything can be done fairly quickly."

"All rights including mineral rights are included?" Ricardo asked.

"Yes. Tomorrow we will begin making the rounds of the offices where it will be necessary to gain approval for the citizenship papers for the two of you. You have additional funds, I hope. You know how business is conducted in Mexico. It always takes money."

"I have enough money to finalize the documents and get the stamps of approval," Ricardo assured him.

Alfredo Garcia looked knowingly at Ricardo. "So you know exactly what is needed. By the way, I forgot to ask you what you want to name the hacienda."

Ricardo looked over at his brother.

"Does it have views?" Rafael asked.

"Yes. It's in the foothills of the mountains."

"Then, let's call it Vista Bonita, beautiful views."

Ricardo nodded his head in agreement. "That's a nice sounding name."

Garcia had a surprised look on his face. "You mean you've never seen the rancho?" he asked Rafael.

Rafael laughed. "Don't look so shocked. I trust my brother. He's even negotiated an agreement with the Apaches next door so that I can keep my scalp."

"Have you met Victoria Barringer?" the lawyer asked.

"No. We've never met. It's nice of her to give me half ownership in a large cattle ranch, though. I do intend to thank her when I meet her."

Garcia looked dumbfounded. Victoria Barringer was never reckless with her money. Giving fifty per cent ownership to a man she had never met did not sound like the woman he knew.

"Mr. Garcia, here's a letter from my grandmother outlining what she wants done. I should have given this to you earlier. It's just to reinforce the paperwork from her that you already have." He handed it to the attorney.

The lawyer read it over quickly and put the letter down. "I'm quite satisfied, but this whole transaction is so unusual. I just wanted to make sure—"

"We understand," said Ricardo. "Each of us will own fifty per cent. The hacienda will be rebuilt and expanded. We are planning to use it as an assembly point for Mexican herds coming from the south. Once they are on Vista Bonita, Arizona cowboys can take the herds from Mexican vaqueros and drive them across the international border to points north. It will be a big operation, and Rafael will head it."

Garcia looked from Ricardo's serious demeanor to Rafael's smiling face.

"I've never run a ranch before. Do you think I will like it?" asked Rafael.

Garcia's eyes widened, and he had a baffled look on his

face.

"My brother is always joking, Mr. Garcia. He is segundo at the Salazar hacienda, and is very experienced in directing operations on a large rancho," Ricardo explained.

The attorney regained his composure quickly. "I knew you were joking," said the smiling lawyer. "Tomorrow night I'm having a dinner party at my home. Probably a dozen people will attend. I would be honored if the two of you would join my wife and me."

"It would be our privilege to join you tomorrow night," Ricardo replied.

"I have reserved a suite for you at the Grand Hotel. Go along the street for a quarter of a mile, then turn left on Juarez Avenue. The hotel will be about three blocks on the right. There is a stable behind the hotel. If you could come here tomorrow morning about nine o'clock, we will begin the citizenship paper process."

The men concluded their meeting and Rafael put his arm around Garcia's shoulder. "On the subject of women, both Ricardo and I are single. Are there places at night that have music and senoritas?"

Garcia grinned. "Horse drawn taxis will be in front of the hotel. They will take you to whatever kind of place you are looking for. I wish I could join you, but when you are married...." He shrugged his shoulders.

***

The following morning Ricardo and Rafael had breakfast in the lavish hotel dining room with its crystal chandeliers and large picture windows looking out on the business community. It was a bustling town where business and pleasure converged, creating a pleasant environment for a variety of appetites.

"You look like death warmed over," Ricardo said.

"You shouldn't have left me. You knew I would get in trouble," Rafael related.

Rafael had bought more than his share of drinks for the surrounding tables at the night clubs, danced with a variety of senoritas, and sang ballads. After midnight, he met a lovely brunette in a red dress. As they prepared to depart in a horse drawn carriage, Ricardo stuffed money in his pocket.

"This should take care of you until morning," Ricardo told him. He watched the carriage depart.

Four hours later a carriage driver dumped the nearly unconscious Rafael on the front steps of the hotel, and employees carried him to his room.

Ricardo couldn't rouse him the next morning. He had the housecleaning staff prepare a hot bath, strip off his clothes, and literally dump him in the tub. This was met with loud bellows from Rafael as he thrashed around in the tub, trying to keep his head above water.

"I'm drowning," he cried out.

Two of the hotel women soaped up the lethargic Mexican and brought a weak smile to his face.

"Come in and join me."

He tried to pull the women into the tub, but they were too fast for him. Later, Ricardo gave him a concoction of vodka, tomato juice, and various sauces, and life began to return for Rafael.

At nine o'clock they arrived at the lawyer's office, and spent the next six hours going from one state office to another in order to have the citizenship papers signed, notarized, and stamped. They received virtually the same treatment at each stop. In order to circumvent the waiting lines of people, Alfredo Garcia would catch the attention of a bureaucrat, shake his hand, and give money to the government employee. Within a few minutes they were called to a private office, where the lawyer would explain the reason for their visit.

"You know this will take several weeks," one bureaucrat pointed out.

Garcia would calmly explain that it was of vital importance that it be done today. Ricardo looked on with interest as the conversation exchange went on for several minutes. Rafael was more than a little on edge from his hangover, and wanted to reach over and grab the bureaucrat by his throat.

The attorney would slip an envelope to the government worker, and he would excuse himself and walk into another room. When he returned, he would smile and note that it would take only a matter of days. Garcia would slip him another envelope, and the same procedure would be followed. The bureaucrat would reappear, take the two sets of papers to another room, and come back with them signed and notarized. Garcia would calmly note that they were not stamped with the official stamp, and slide another envelope across the table. The manager would excuse himself, and would return later with the proper stamp in place.

Rafael was edgy, had a bad hangover, and was short tempered.

"Why don't you just give him all of the money in one envelope? It would be a lot simpler," he pointed out.

"There are two reasons," Garcia reasoned. "We may be able to get one of these bureaucrats to accept a lesser amount. You don't want to pay more than you have to. Secondly, if you give him a large amount up front, he will think you are an easy touch for another large envelope filled with money."

By noon they had obtained two out of three official stamps necessary to legalize the citizenship papers. No one had asked where Ricardo or Rafael was born, because no one cared.

The three men sat down for lunch at the hotel, and Ricardo excused himself and walked to the bathroom. He headed down a long hallway, beautifully carpeted with mirrors on both walls, and stopped when he heard voices.

The mirror next to him reflected the images of two men in a side hallway. One man was tall, dignified, and wore an expensive suit. The second was a short, thin, little man wearing the uniform of a servant. The small man reached inside the suit coat of his employer and fondled his private parts. This brought a smile to the gentleman's face. Ricardo was frozen in place, feeling as if he was eavesdropping. Finally, the tall man looked to one side, saw Ricardo in the mirror, and pushed the little man away. He looked at Ricardo a second time and smiled.

Ricardo continued his walk to the bathroom. *That bastard thought I might be interested*, he reasoned.

When he returned to the table, Rafael was eating bread and salad as fast as he could chew, attempting to settle his stomach. "This food is excellent," he proclaimed, and grinned.

The gentleman from the hallway and his man servant seated themselves at a table near the far end of the dining room. Garcia saw them and stood up.

"Excuse me. I need to say hello to a gentleman over there. I will be back in a moment." Garcia spent less than a minute exchanging pleasantries with the man across the room, and then returned.

"You will meet him this evening. He and his fiancée are in town and will be at our home for dinner. His name is Miguel Soto, and he comes from a very wealthy family with extensive mining interests here and on the west coast of Mexico."

Good luck to his bride, Ricardo thought. *She'll have to share the bed with the man servant.*

CHAPTER 10

As the carriage stopped in front of Alfredo Garcia's home atop a hill overlooking Hermosillo, the Montoya brothers were immediately impressed. The exterior of the house bore a strong resemblance to a French colonial mansion, three stories tall, including a full basement. The hipped roof, covered with wooden shingles, dominated the entire structure.

A wide veranda extended around all four sides, corners supported by delicate colonnettes that tied into porch railings with interlocking wooden designs. The elevated veranda rested upon heavy brick pillars, raised in order to allow light into the basement windows. Six dormer windows allowed light into the second story rooms, and four rectangular chimneys extended above the roof. The veranda and interior rooms all had shiny wood floors. Brick for the outer walls had been fired in kilns at the rear of the home. Exterior doors and trim were of California redwood, beautiful in color and noted for durability.

The Montoya brothers walked up the stairs to the veranda and were greeted by the owner.

"Your home is most impressive," said Ricardo.

79

"Can I build one like this at Vista Bonita?" Rafael asked jokingly.

"I had much of the materials sent by boat from San Francisco, and also many of the furnishings," Garcia explained.

The living room exhibited redwood walls, the like of which the Montoya brothers had never seen, gorgeous tapestries, beautiful paintings, and a huge Oriental rug covering the center of the room. Furniture, chairs, and couches were situated around all four walls. A dozen men and women were drinking champagne and other liquors. Garcia introduced the brothers to the other guests as they walked around the room.

Ricardo recognized Miguel Soto immediately. The woman standing next to him had her head turned, talking with another lady. Garcia introduced the brothers to Soto and they shook hands, Soto smiling at Ricardo in recognition. The young woman was dressed in a shimmering light blue gown cut low in front, and had her head turned.

"Christina Aragon, I would like you to meet Ricardo and Rafael Montoya. They are purchasing a rancho in the general area of your uncle's hacienda," said Garcia.

The woman turned and looked into Ricardo's eyes. Montoya felt as if a knife had been thrust into his stomach.

Christina Aragon had dark, curly, shoulder length hair that framed a light complexioned oval face. Her high cheek bones, smooth skin, long neck, and large, strikingly beautiful blue eyes were captivating. Christina's voluptuous figure was accented by full breasts, a thin waist, and long legs.

Her piercing, almost hypnotic stare went straight through Ricardo. The couple continued to stare at one another for several seconds. Neither one would look away, as if they were frozen in time.

Rafael glanced at his brother and then back at Christina.

This is a little embarrassing, he thought. *That's another man's fiancée*. "I'm pleased to meet you," said Rafael, in an effort to break his brother's trance.

She glanced at Rafael, smiled, and then returned her gaze to Ricardo. "Why haven't we met before?" she asked in a low sensual voice.

Ricardo had recovered enough to manage a reply. "I've only been to Hermosillo a few times to sell cattle."

The tinkling of a bell signaled that dinner awaited the guests. The people slowly filed into a large, formal dining room with three massive chandeliers above a long table. The candle lights reflected off gorgeous china, beautiful silverware, and fragile glassware. Around the perimeter of the room were hung a dozen lanterns, creating a blaze of light.

An older gentleman was about to sit next to Christina when Ricardo approached him and asked if he would like to sit next to Alfredo Garcia. The elderly man was happy to oblige. He wanted to talk business with Garcia, anyway.

***

The couple was oblivious to their surroundings. Christina seemed entranced by the tall, very handsome Mexican with a broad face, high forehead, strong nose, and granite-like chin. His dark eyes never wavered when he looked at her, and she felt a strange awakening within. She wanted to reach out and touch him, knowing she would be safe in his arms.

The dinner progressed course after course with fine foods. Christina and Ricardo ate little as they chatted and looked into each other's eyes. Trouble came from a source that no one would have imagined. Seated next to Rafael and directly opposite Christina and Ricardo was her maiden aunt, Olivia Aragon.

***

"Where are you from, Mr. Montoya?" Olivia asked in a scratchy voice.

Ricardo looked across the table, seeing her for the first time.

"I think you were introduced. But she is my Aunt Olivia," Christina said.

Ricardo's eyes widened. *Another aunt*, he thought. *Why does every beautiful woman have an aunt guarding her?*

"I was raised in northern Mexico to the northwest of Hermosillo," he replied. "I was born in the United States, but came to Mexico as a baby."

"Were your parents Mexican?"

Ricardo looked at Rafael. His brother studied the chandelier.

"My birth parents were Anglos. But the only parents I ever knew were my Mexican parents who raised me."

"Then you are really a gringo," she said in a nasty, disrespectful tone of voice.

"I have dual citizenship, both from the United States and Mexico."

"But you are really a gringo!" she emphasized in a loud obnoxious manner, designed to intimidate and provoke.

Ricardo looked over at Christina and immediately remembered to be diplomatic in his response. He wanted to choke the old lady, but instead smiled at her. Everyone at the table had stopped talking, fascinated by the exchange.

"I'll give you the basic background on my heritage. My Anglo parents were killed in an ambush of their carriage in the Arizona Territory. My mother hid me in the rocks before she was killed. My Mexican father was camped nearby and witnessed where she hid me. Risking his life, he worked his way down the hillside that was covered with boulders, picked me up, and ran back to his camp. He took me to Mexico and raised me as his son, alongside Rafael. It wasn't until my father, Gustavo, was dying that he told me the truth. He said he had to clear his conscience before he passed on."

The people around the table were all staring at Ricardo. No one made a sound. Even Aunt Olivia seemed intrigued by the story.

"So, in answer to your question, I am really a Mexican."

"What is your Anglo name? Did you ever find out?" she hissed.

If I could just get my hands around your neck, he thought. "Yes, my name in the Arizona Territory is James Barringer."

Then she asked the question to which everyone wanted to know the answer.

"Did you find out who killed your parents?" she asked slyly.

"Yes," he said in a hard voice. "Now all of them are dead."

Alfredo Garcia interceded. "Gentlemen, why don't we go to my study for cigars and brandy?" he announced. There was a shuffling of chairs as the ladies and gentlemen rose to leave the room.

"Meet me on the veranda in about ten minutes," Ricardo said quietly to Christina.

"Yes," she replied, not really thinking, just reacting to the magnetism of the moment.

In the study, the men sat down comfortably in supple leather chairs spread in a half circle around the room. The conversation centered on cattle and mining in the area. In ten minutes Ricardo excused himself, walked out of the room, and down the hallway toward the bathroom. Then he changed course and walked out onto the back veranda. The back yard was a huge flower garden that stretched for fifty yards, and lanterns hung from branches, giving the flowering trees a soft illumination.

***

Christina Aragon walked onto the veranda, almost gliding as she moved. "Are you always so direct?" she asked quietly. The soft backyard light accented her light skin and sparkling eyes.

"Always," he replied.

Ricardo's eyes narrowed with desire and determination. He moved to her and put his hands on her shoulders, pulling her to him. He kissed her with a passion that startled and aroused her simultaneously. After a moment's hesitation, she put her arms around him and responded strongly. They were caught up in the intense emotional excitement of the moment, blocking out all decorum and propriety.

"I never expected anything like this," she said softly, trying to catch her breath. He kissed her again and she felt dizzy, lost in his arms, not wanting to stop.

Ricardo's arms wrapped around her, holding Christina tightly. "Sometimes two people are just meant to be together. The two of us are that way," he said quietly. "I never want to let you go."

She took him by the hand and led him into the flower garden, where they were shielded by trees.

"You know I'm engaged. Our two families have mutual business interests, and this marriage is meant to solidify the relationship," she lamented with scant sincerity.

Ricardo kissed her gently on the cheek, neck, and then on the lips. Christina made a slight moaning sound. Ricardo was not interested in anything but the passion of the moment and wanting to possess the woman in his arms. He began moving his hands over her body, causing her to shudder.

"I've got to go back. My aunt will be hunting for me," she whispered, fighting off her own sexual desire that came bursting to the surface.

"Are you staying at the hotel?" he asked.

"Yes. It's a two bedroom suite, and Aunt Olivia has the other bedroom," she replied, amazed at her own bold, presumptuous response.

"I'm staying in room two hundred, and my brother is not staying with me. Come when you can get away," he whispered in her ear.

"I don't know if I can."

"Do it," he said softly. "I've never had this feeling of magnetism before, and I can tell you feel the same."

He took her in his arms again, kissed her, and felt an incredible desire to possess Christina, his craving bordering on lust. She responded in the same manner, holding him tightly, not wanting to let go.

There was a call from the porch. "Christina. Where are you?" the scratchy voice of Aunt Olivia called out.

"I've got to go!" she moaned.

"I'll be waiting later tonight."

"All right," she replied softly as she gasped for breath.

Christina broke loose, hurried across the grass, and climbed the veranda stairs. *What am I doing?* she thought. *I've never felt this way before.*

Aunt Olivia could see a man's legs near the base of an orange tree. "That Miguel Soto, such an impetuous young man."

"Yes. He certainly is," Christina noted.

***

Ricardo returned to the study. The conversation was still on mining and cattle, but it passed over his head as he dreamed of the night ahead. An hour later the carriages began to pick up the dinner guests.

Rafael shook Alfredo Garcia's hand. "Your house is one of the most beautiful I have ever seen. And your hospitality was fabulous."

Garcia and the Montoya brothers agreed to meet again the following day at his office to finalize the sales agreement and finish the visits to the governmental offices needed to legitimize the citizenship and contract papers.

As the coach pulled away, Rafael looked at his brother. "What are you doing? You have lipstick on your mouth. That whole group of men knew that you two had been together. Soto acted as if he didn't care. What the hell is wrong with him?"

Ricardo took out a handkerchief and wiped his mouth. "I didn't know who Soto was when I saw him in a hallway at the hotel. His servant was fondling his balls in a back hallway, and he liked it."

Rafael's eyes widened and his mouth fell open. "Mother of God!"

"Christina Aragon is all I can think about," Ricardo admitted. "I've never felt this way about any woman."

Rafael stared at his brother in the half light. "It's usually me who's getting in trouble over women, not you."

"I could tell she feels the same…I could feel it," Ricardo asserted.

Rafael's eyes narrowed. "Do you think she knows about Soto fooling around with men?"

"No. I don't think she has any idea."

Rafael was quiet for a moment, lost in thought. "What are you going to do?"

"Try to reason with her to break off the engagement."

"That won't be easy. When you were gone, the conversation was about the coming marriage solidifying a bond between the two families. His father is bringing a great deal of money to invest in Aragon's mines. She never met Miguel before she arrived from Spain. This is strictly business, and if you screw that up, they will come after you."

"I gave her my room number. She will come later."

"Well, I hope my snoring doesn't bother her. That's my room too."

"Find yourself another room," Ricardo said, and laughed.

Rafael grinned. "Be careful brother. These Spaniards still believe in duels."

When they returned to the hotel, Rafael paid for another room. He immediately started a conversation with a young female employee, who he coaxed into showing him where the room was located. He smiled at Ricardo as he and the young woman went up the stairs. She began laughing when Rafael patted her on the butt. *That's my brother*, Ricardo thought.

He paced the room for the next hour, but there was no knock on the door. Ricardo lay down on the bed, thrashing around, unable to rest. He threw open the glass and iron doors leading out to the balcony and walked outside. Christina's room was 302, one story up and one room to the right. He stood there looking at the lighted room above. After a moment's hesitation, Ricardo climbed onto the railing outside his room and pulled himself up to the railing of the balcony above him. The room was dark.

The distance between the half circle railings was a little more than four feet in width. Ricardo climbed over the railing and reached across the opening to the railing around the French doors in Christina's room, but the distance was too far. *I'll have to jump*, he thought. *It's the only way.*

Ricardo was sweating profusely as he pushed off and jumped, grabbing the railing outside Christina's suite. There was a sharp metallic wrenching sound as the bolts pulled loose from the building. He crash-landed on the balcony floor and kicked a metal table across the balcony, which smashed into the railing on the other side. The sounds echoed loudly.

***

Inside the room, Christina was sitting in a chair with her face in her hands. She jumped up, startled by the loud noise, and saw Ricardo picking himself up off the balcony floor.

"What happened, Christina?" Aunt Olivia yelled from the second bedroom.

"Nothing, Aunt Olivia. I just dropped a tray on the patio. Go back to sleep."

"All right. But, please be careful."

Ricardo stood there panting. Christina put a finger to her lips, walked over to her aunt's room, and listened intently. The soft snoring began again as she closed the door.

Christina turned to Ricardo. "What are you doing?"

"I had to see you, and I didn't want to knock on the door."

"My aunt locked the door and took the key to bed with her," Christina whispered.

They suddenly grasped the humor in the situation, and both began laughing as quietly as they could. He pulled her to him and the two of them were concerned only about the present and their mutual desire. Locked in each other's arms, the big man overwhelmed the beautiful woman, and minutes later they were in her bedroom. Ricardo and Christiana made love twice before they were in a mood to talk, caught up in their desire for one another. Her body looked almost translucent, smooth and beautiful in the dim light through the window.

"If you keep running your hand over me, I won't be able

to speak," she said softly.

"I want you to break off the engagement. I'm in love with you, and I want to marry you."

"We've just met. This is all so crazy. I must have lost my mind," she lamented.

"Do you feel the same about me?"

"Yes, or I wouldn't be here right now."

"Sometimes two people meet and they feel an overwhelming attraction for each other. That's what I feel for you, and I think you feel the same about me."

Christina sighed. "I do."

"I could be around another woman for months or years and not have this feeling. It's sudden, rushing at us all at once, but it's real and will be lasting," he assured her.

"If I was to suddenly break off the engagement, the Sotos would be disgraced. Spanish families have a great deal of pride."

"And arrogance," he added.

"Well yes, but my family's reputation is at stake. We're planning to visit my uncle's hacienda in northern Mexico this week. Uncle Ramon Aragon is arriving tomorrow to take us to his hacienda. It's probably not far from the rancho you are buying. He has property that the Sotos and my father, Franco, want to develop for mining. Supposedly, it's rich in gold and silver."

"But, you don't love Miguel Soto. You've barely met him. Why is the marriage so important?"

"It's our culture, you know that. A marriage cements two families together. An arranged marriage, such as this one, is common among wealthy families in Spain and Mexico. In this case, it brings the two countries together, as well as the families."

"What were your feelings when you were told about the planned marriage?"

"Shock, I suppose. I knew that some type of planned marriage would take place because I never found a man in Spain who I wanted to marry."

Ricardo reflected on her explanation and was deep in thought.

"Have you ever met my uncle, Ramon Aragon?" she asked.

"Yes, I've met Don Ramon," he said unenthusiastically.

***

She waited for him to elaborate, but Ricardo was silent, thinking about Don Ramon Aragon and his friendship with the late Don Diego Salazar. They had socialized together at parties and holiday celebrations, womanizing and bragging about their tyrannical treatment of peons. The two dons believed savage brutality brought obedience, and they often exercised this prerogative. Don Ramon would glare at Montoya because of Ricardo's direct, unflinching stare, and total lack of subservience.

"I haven't seen him since I was a child," she stated. "What is your impression of him?"

Ricardo knew better than to tell her the truth. It would not be good to assassinate the don's character when Christina was about to become his guest, Ricardo surmised.

"He was a friend of my previous employer, Don Diego Salazar. I met him on several occasions, usually at holiday parties. I really don't know the man very well."

Christina guessed he was being diplomatic. She kissed him and said, "I think you are trying to be polite."

"I'll let you make up your own mind about your uncle," he said, and smiled.

She asked questions about his background and previous life. Ricardo found himself telling her everything about his life on El Rancho Grande, his determination to discover his heritage, and the events that led up to his arrival in Hermosillo. Christina was fascinated and plied him with more and more questions. Finally, he began kissing her again and the questions ceased. They watched the daybreak and made plans to meet in his room that evening. She would make sure to get an extra key to her room, she promised. Christina quietly entered her aunt's bedroom, but could not find the key to let Ricardo out of the suite. Aunt Olivia must have it on her person, she told him. "It's getting light," she pointed out.

Ricardo sighed. "I know. I just don't want to leave you."

"If Aunt Olivia wakes up and finds you here...."

He kissed her, walked over to the balcony, and looked down. "I should be able to get to the balcony below."

They held each other one last time, and he began the downward climb. Ricardo hung from the creaking balcony, his boots touched the railing just below him. But a portion of the railing he was holding broke off, sending the piece flying onto the next balcony with the clatter of iron hitting iron. Ricardo lost his balance, bent down, and managed to grab the iron railing on the second floor. It ripped loose from the building, the iron structure hanging down, leaving him dangling ten feet above the boardwalk and street.

Christina was horrified as she watched the scene unfold. The crash and clatter of noise brought her aunt running out of her bedroom.

"What's going on?" Aunt Olivia yelled.

A fat bell boy came out of the hotel and looked up at Ricardo hanging from the piece of wrought iron. It gave way and pulled loose, sending Montoya down on top of the hotel employee. There was another crash and clatter as the iron fabrication hit the ground next to them. The bell boy had the wind knocked out of him, but Ricardo was unhurt. He waved at Christina and hurried into the hotel.

"Don't go out on the balcony! It's falling apart. It's not safe," Christina warned her aunt.

"The hotel management will hear about this. It's falling to pieces. What kind of a hotel is this, anyway?" she yelled in her scratchy voice.

Hotel employees were hurrying out onto the boardwalk, and helped the bell boy to his feet. People began to gather, looking up at the two damaged balconies. The hotel manager had just arrived for work, and Ricardo grabbed him by the arm.

"It's my fault. But we need to keep this quiet. There's a lady's reputation at stake," he declared.

Ricardo pulled money from his pocket and gave the manager enough to buy ten new balconies.

"Keep the rest for yourself," he said quietly.

The manager looked at the money and his eyes widened.

"It will remain our secret," he said and smiled. "Are you all right?"

"I'm fine," said a grinning Ricardo.

Montoya took the stairs two at a time, unlocked the door, and entered his room, falling face down on the bed, asleep in an instant.

CHAPTER 11

The Montoya brothers entered Alfredo Garcia's law office shortly after noon. The attorney greeted them dressed impeccably in his usual black suit, string tie, and starched white shirt, reflecting the image of a successful lawyer. Rafael had red, puffy eyes. Ricardo was sore all over from the fall. Neither man felt much like talking, but they thanked him again for the wonderful dinner party.

"This is a set of originals of your birth certifications. Additional sets of originals go to the three state offices involved, and I will keep another set here just in case we need them. As soon as I receive the remainder of the money for the sale, I'll finalize a number of sets of contract papers. One set will be sent to Victoria Barringer, one will be on file here, and additional sets will go to the previous owner, Don Jorge Franco, and to the state offices," Garcia explained.

"That sounds like a lot of copies," said Rafael.

"I have an office full of young ladies to make those copies."

"And a nice group they are," Rafael noted, grinning.

"When we leave here, Rafael will go to Vista Bonita to assess the amount of remodeling and rebuilding that will be needed," Ricardo explained.

"Is our end of it complete?" Rafael asked.

"Yes. There are no other papers to sign. I have your powers of attorney, and I will take care of the rest. I'm not going to make you go through the same routine of going from office to office to get the official stamps. I'll do it myself," Garcia stated.

"In that case, I will catch a little nap before dinner," Rafael said. He shook hands with Garcia and walked out, but not before giving admiring glances to the young ladies in the office and receiving smiles in return.

"Rafael is having a great time. He's been stuck on the Salazar rancho for too long. This is a refreshing change for him," Ricardo explained.

"And for you," Garcia said, and gave Montoya a knowing glance.

"You heard about the balconies and railings coming down?" Montoya asked.

"No one could figure out what happened, and the hotel manager isn't talking."

Ricardo briefly described what had occurred, but left out Christina's name. Garcia just shook his head and laughed. "Ah, to be young again." The attorney looked through his window into the main legal department and frowned. "Have you met Don Ramon Aragon? He's arrived, but we'll let him wait."

"I would think we have the same opinion of the man."

Garcia looked at Montoya with a serious expression on his face. "Be careful. Miguel Soto has killed a couple of men in duels in Spain. Don Ramon is committed to this marriage, so there will be a union of the two families. The Sotos and the Aragons are powerful families in Mexico and Spain."

The lawyer continued. "I like both you and your brother.

Both of you have character, and I can tell that you treat others with respect. I, myself, came from a peon background. You carry that stigma with you until you rise to a high level in society. Even now, the dons look upon me as not being their equal because I was born poor."

Montoya smiled. "That's interesting. Looking at you and your magnificent home, I would never have guessed that you came from a peon background. As I mentioned at your house, my parents were peons on the Salazar ranch. My brother and I were both chosen to be educated, taught English, and schooled in the art of firearms. I rose to the rank of segundo at an early age. Rafael became head of Don Diego's private army."

"Both of us have risen to heights that our parents would never have expected," said Garcia. "You explained before about learning who your true parents were and being an heir to the Barringer Empire. It must be strange being a different man in two countries."

"I'm getting used to it," Ricardo responded.

"Just be careful while you are here. Anyone who is around you and Christina can tell that you are infatuated with one another. I noticed it at the dinner table last night. Strangely, Miguel Soto didn't seem to care."

Ricardo looked Garcia in the eye. "That's because he likes men, not women. His valet is more than a man servant."

Garcia sat back in his chair and exhaled loudly. He shook his head from side to side as he stared at Ricardo. "Christina is so beautiful and so nice. Condemning her to a marriage like that is preposterous!"

"It's all about money."

"What are you going to do?"

Montoya sighed. "Do you have any ideas?"

"Let me think about it," said the lawyer. "I'll bring Don

Ramon in so the two of you can become reacquainted."

Ricardo nodded in agreement. Garcia went to the outer office and greeted Don Ramon in a friendly manner. They talked for a few moments, and then the lawyer brought him into his private office.

Aragon was very short, fat, had a round face with large eyes, and the top of his head was bald. The hair above his ears and around the back of his head was shoulder length and held together in a ponytail. He wore a dark blue suit with gold buttons and a flowery white shirt.

Don Ramon's greeting was short, gruff, and did not include a handshake. Montoya had experienced it before, a short, fat man instinctively disliking a tall, handsome man.

"I wanted you two to meet again. Ricardo and his brother are purchasing the rancho owned by Don Jorge Franco. We just concluded the contracts," Garcia said.

"Franco had no stomach for it. Lots of Indians, but no stomach for a fight. I would have brought the federal army in and done away with the whole lot of them," Aragon snarled. "Franco ran instead." The don tried to mask his dislike for Ricardo, remembering their previous encounters, but his eyes were revealing.

"We are going to use the property for a staging area for cattle herds. At that point, we can substitute Arizona cowboys for the vaqueros and drive the herds north to the railroad in Tucson," Montoya explained.

"How many cattle?" the little man growled as he brushed off his flowery white shirt and smoothed his blue suit.

Montoya and Garcia exchanged glances. "Perhaps one hundred thousand or more per year," said Ricardo.

Don Ramon blew air out of his mouth and grunted. "That's absurd!" His lips were sealed tightly, the corners of his mouth turned down in a perpetual frown.

"He just paid cash for the Franco hacienda," Garcia pointed out.

The fat man's eyes widened. "Really! Did you strike it rich after you left Don Diego?"

"My grandmother owns about sixty thousand acres in the Arizona Territory, and has another thirty thousand under lease for timber and mining operations," Ricardo said in a calm, level voice.

A marked change of character suddenly came over the little rancher. His eyes lit up, and he smiled at the thought of ensnaring Montoya in one of his investment schemes. "Well, we will have to talk some more. I have some wonderful Mexican investments to discuss with you."

"My brother and I are leaving to go to our new ranch tomorrow or the next day. It's unfortunate that we can't spend more time together," Montoya stated. "I would like to hear about your investment opportunities."

Aragon's eyes sparkled. "Well, my niece and her fiancé will be accompanying me back to the ranch, probably tomorrow or the next day. Why don't you come with us and spend a few days at my rancho?"

"It won't be an imposition?" Ricardo asked.

"Oh, no, no, no. I would be overjoyed if you would come with us."

"I'll talk it over with my brother, but I think it sounds like an excellent idea." Ricardo stood up. "I know you two want to discuss business, so I will talk with you later."

Don Ramon grabbed Ricardo's hand and shook it vigorously. Garcia smiled at how smoothly Montoya had wangled an invitation that would allow him to be near Christina Aragon for the next few days, or possibly even weeks.

***

That evening the two brothers were finishing dinner and sipping wine in the hotel dining room. "I've never liked cities, but I sure could get used to this. There are women all over the place. It's like picking oranges off a tree," said Rafael. The men joked, laughed, and enjoyed themselves for the next hour, drinking one brandy after another. "Tell me, brother. Have you decided what to do about Soto and Christina?" Rafael asked.

Ricardo pondered the question. "If I tell her, she might think that I was purposely trying to break up the engagement for my own benefit. If I don't tell her, I would be letting her continue forward into an unnatural marriage, one she would detest when she found out."

"Do you want me to shoot him?"

Ricardo jerked upright in his seat. "Of course not!"

Rafael started laughing. "I'm just kidding."

Miguel Soto walked into the dining room as the brothers were preparing to leave. The tall, dark complected man was dressed in an immaculate suit and had a serious look on his face. He walked over to the brothers' table.

"I would like to speak with you," he said quietly to Ricardo.

"I'm just leaving. It's time to search for the evening's entertainment," Rafael announced as he got up from the table and departed, ignoring Soto. He threw his brother a backward glance and a sly grin as he left.

"Please sit down," Ricardo stated. Soto sat down opposite Montoya.

"These conversations are always delicate but need to be discussed," said the Spaniard.

"Feel free to proceed," Ricardo stated.

"The marriage between Christina and me was arranged by our families. It is most important that the marriage take place next month. A lot of planning, time, and effort have gone into this arrangement. Large amounts of money will change hands when contracts are signed," Soto explained. "Nothing must stand in the way of these contracts moving forward."

"There are a couple of problems, of course," Montoya emphasized. "Number one is that you don't love her, and secondly you are attracted to men, not women. Do you really think she would marry you if she found out?"

Soto's eyes narrowed, and a look of fury twisted his facial features, never having been spoken to in such a manner. "In my country, Spain, I would challenge you to a duel for such an insult," he growled.

"In my country, Mexico, I would knock you on your ass," Ricardo stated in a strong voice.

The two men stared at each other unflinchingly. Soto began to calm down, realizing that his actions could cause everything to blow up in his face. "Look, Montoya, arranged marriages occur in Spain and in Mexico all the time. This is nothing new. And, the partners in the marriages often lead separate lives, free to do whatever they please."

Ricardo's eyes narrowed, his face mirroring disgust. "Usually both parties are aware of the rules of conduct before they enter into such a marriage. That isn't the case here," said Montoya. His voice was hard and his demeanor was unrelenting.

"This marriage is none of your business. Stay out of it," Soto warned.

"I haven't said anything to her about your preference for men. But I am in love with her, and I will try to convince her to break the engagement and marry me," Ricardo said in a harsh, cutting voice.

A look of loathing came over Soto's face. "I despise men like you. You sicken me with your stupid sense of moral superiority. If you do anything to harm these business deals...." The Spaniard stopped short of threatening to kill Ricardo.

Montoya's jaw was firm, his eyes narrowed, and his face took on a granite-like appearance. "You had better go. We don't have anything more to talk about."

***

The Spaniard stood up slowly, turned, and walked away, neither man knowing what to do. Soto walked up the hotel stairs to the second floor and knocked on Aunt Olivia's door. Christina opened it, smiling at her fiancé. "Hello Miguel. I'm surprised to see you."

"Christina, I wonder if we could talk in private," he said in a smooth, soft voice. Soto was charming, debonair, and persuasive when he wanted to be, and his target was the beautiful brunette standing in front of him.

"Yes. Come in. Aunt Olivia is visiting friends and won't be back for a while."

***

When they were seated on a couch, Miguel touched her arm in a loving manner. "I am very happy with our engagement. I never believed you could be so beautiful and charming."

Christina was taken aback and looked surprised because of his previous lack of interest.

"I realize the marriage was arranged. But I think we will be very happy together. Both of our families are very proud of us. And I think you are a wonderful person," he said, and smiled.

She wondered what had brought this on. He had been very distant in all of their meetings since she had arrived from Spain.

"I don't want to lose you for any reason," Soto stated. "I want to spend the rest of my life with you, and hopefully we will have children and a great life."

Christina felt confused and bewildered. *Why hasn't he said something like this before?* she mused. *Why now?*

"There might be those who would try to break up the engagement. I don't want that to happen for any reason," he said in a quiet, respectful tone of voice.

She suddenly felt an uneasiness pass over her. "What do you mean?"

"As you know, in Europe, the upper classes have an open-mindedness and are more liberally permissive when it comes to liaisons between people of the same sex. I, myself, experimented with things of that nature in my earlier years. It was never important, it just happened. But I want you to know that I am totally committed to our marriage as man and wife."

Christina was shocked, almost speechless. "Why are you telling me this? What brought this on?"

"There are those who might come to you and say things with the express purpose of breaking up our engagement. I don't want anything to tear us apart," he said in a soft, sincere voice. "I am totally committed to you."

Because he broached the subject, Christina looked him in the eyes and asked the question now uppermost in her mind. "Are you still involved with men?"

"No. It was just an experimental phase that some young men go through. It never really meant anything. It ended a long time ago. But I try never to hide the truth, especially if it might be used against me."

Christina studied his face, searching for the truth. "Well, I appreciate your forthright manner. But who would use something like that against you."

"I think you know. I'm not blind. I see that you and Montoya are developing a relationship. You are not my wife yet, so I really can not stop you or curtail your freedom of decision."

Christina's mind was in turmoil. "Please give me some time to think about this."

"Of course. I do want our marriage to work. I'm committed to being an honest, forthright husband," he said quietly. "Good night."

Soto stood up and walked towards the door. Christina was too shocked to move. After the door closed, she put her head against the back of the couch and sighed. *What am I going to do?*

Aunt Olivia returned to the room a few minutes later. "It's enjoyable being with relatives, but I am tired," she announced. She readied herself for bed and then yelled from the bedroom. "Don't go out on the balcony. I still don't think it's safe even though they repaired it."

"Yes, Aunt Olivia."

Within minutes her aunt was asleep. Christina waited another half hour before she left the suite and locked the door. She walked up the flight of stairs to the third floor and went directly to Ricardo's room. When she knocked, Ricardo opened the door immediately. They gazed steadily at one another and their intense looks told of their inner feelings. She rushed forward and they wrapped their arms around each other. He lifted her off her feet and carried her into his bedroom.

They made love quickly and then lay in each other's

arms, content and not wanting to move, talking about small things, neither one wanting to discuss the main topic that was uppermost in their minds, the coming marriage.

Finally, she decided it was time. "Miguel came to my room this evening. He said people might try to discredit him, and he wanted to tell me about his early life."

"I see, go on," he replied, sweat popping out on his body.

"He said he experimented with men. I know other men in Spain have done the same. It's craziness, but young men do strange things. However, he pledged his love and said that was in the past, and he wanted children and a happy marriage to me. He seemed sincere."

Soto is a smart man, Ricardo thought. *He's covering his tracks.*

"His valet is his lover."

Christina was startled and sat up in bed. "You knew about this!" she blurted out.

"I did, and I know for a fact that his man servant is his lover," Ricardo said quietly.

"Well, when were you going to tell me?" she said in a hurt voice.

"I've been struggling with that question. If I tell you, you might think I'm making it up to destroy the engagement. If I don't tell you, I'm condemning you to a loveless marriage. It's a no win situation for me," he explained. "I finally decided to try hard to convince you to end the engagement. If that didn't work, I would have told you."

She lay down flat on her back and emitted a sound of utter frustration. "Please leave, Ricardo. I have to think this through on my own."

"You're in my room."

"Oh," she exclaimed, sitting up and moving quickly to put on her clothes.

103

"Christina, let's talk about this. It's very important," he said as he pulled on his pants.

She fixed him with a level gaze. "This all happened so quickly. I need a little time to think through everything that you and Miguel have told me. It's not that I doubt your honesty, I just need time to organize my thoughts."

Ricardo was at a loss for words as she let herself out and closed the door.

CHAPTER 12

The trip north from Hermosillo to Don Ramon Aragon's Rancho Verde hacienda was accomplished in an elaborately decorated coach that held Christina Aragon, Aunt Olivia Aragon, Miguel Soto, and Don Ramon. Six mounted bodyguards and two men atop the carriage plus the Montoya brothers rounded out the group. Ricardo and Rafael deferred the offer to ride inside, claiming that they would like to scout the trail ahead and the foothills nearby for signs of Apaches. In reality, neither man wanted to feel Aunt Olivia's looks of dislike and Don Ramon's constant barrage of investment opportunities.

Christina and Ricardo barely spoke during first day of the trip. Don Ramon explained to his passengers that he wanted to discuss business with the Montoya brothers when they reached his rancho, and this was the reason they were accompanying the coach. When the group would stop for a break, she would engage Miguel in conversation. Soto was a complete gentleman, smiling and attending to her every need. He had left his valet in Hermosillo, and Christina was beginning to question Ricardo's story about the two men and their liaison. Miguel would hold her hand, show affection, and continually converse with Christina.

The Montoya brothers were soon caught up in problems of another sort. There were signs indicating a large number of Apaches were in the area. As they scouted into the foothills, the brothers came upon a recent Apache camp, and studied the campfire sites, footprints, and where the horses had been tethered.

"How many would you guess?" Ricardo asked his brother.

Rafael thought for a moment. "I'd say forty or more. It's a large raiding party."

"You think there are that many?" Ricardo asked.

"Yes. They had more than one campfire, so the number of men was substantial. Also, the number of hoof prints would indicate a large group of horses."

The brothers caught up to the coach and signaled for it to stop. "What's the problem?" asked Don Ramon as he climbed down from the carriage.

"There's a large number of Apaches near here, possibly forty or more. It's one of the largest raiding parties I've encountered in recent months," Ricardo observed.

The don's face lost its color, and his mouth dropped open. "What are we going to do?" he said in a desperate tone of voice.

"Santa Ana is near here. We were going to stop there for the night, but I think it would be a good idea to continue on to your rancho. We can warn the people there and then get moving again," said Ricardo.

"Let's not stop. Let's just keep going. The sooner we get to my rancho and have the protection of more men, the safer I will feel," Aragon blurted out, eyes wide with fear.

"I agree with him. Let's keep moving," Aunt Olivia hissed,

her head sticking out of the coach window.

"The coach can keep going, but Ricardo and I will warn the peons and shop keepers," said Rafael.

"I want your protection," Don Ramon protested.

Rafael was furious at the don's lack of decency towards the townspeople. "I'm not going to tell you again, we will stop and warn the people. Now, get back in your coach and let's get going!" Rafael ordered.

Don Ramon scrambled back into the coach without another word. They picked up the pace and entered the two-street town an hour later. The brothers took less than fifteen minutes to warn the families in the small community. Peons went running to the nearby adobe houses to warn others and bring them into the confines of Santa Anna. In all, about sixty men, women, and children were banding together. Apaches did not like to attack large numbers of Mexicans, preferring to strike ranchos or tiny communities during the early morning hours when they could butcher the half-asleep families. Most of the men living in and around Santa Ana were armed and the element of surprise was gone, so the war party would move on to easier victims, the Montoyas reasoned. The coach stayed in town until Ricardo and Rafael were ready to leave.

"They are taking too much time," Don Ramon lamented, sweating profusely.

"They are just peons and store keepers. They can be replaced at a moment's notice," Soto proclaimed as he looked out the coach's window. For the moment he had forgotten his pretext of civility and generosity, which did not go unnoticed by Christina.

"Who cares about them? They are just servants and workers. Let's get moving!" Aunt Olivia exclaimed, her scratchy voice loud and demanding.

Christina gazed at Miguel Soto. His true character had come to the surface, and she realized that he cared nothing about the common man. He glanced at her as she studied him, realizing his blunder.

"I really did not mean that, Christina. I'm sorry," he said in a sincere voice. "The danger about us —"

"You don't need to explain," she replied.

Rafael rode up to the carriage. "All right, let's get moving."

That night the moon was full and lighted the trail, and they made good time, stopping only to rest the horses once every hour. It was dawn when they sighted Rancho Verde's headquarters at the center of a compound of buildings. Aragon's large, white, two-story rancho had outside balconies running around two sides of the second floor, the upper level comprising Don Ramon's private residence. Smaller buildings encircled a large courtyard in front of the balcony. Aragon would stand on the balcony and give orders to the assembled workers, vaqueros, and peons, addressing them like vassals each morning.

The coach unloaded near the stairs. "Come up for a moment. I want you to see the interior of the hacienda. I have done extensive decorating," Don Ramon said excitedly.

The guests were tired and wanted to sleep, but trudged up the stairs to the second floor. They turned and looked out into the courtyard, viewing a man tied to the side of a small building. One of Aragon's vaqueros ran up the stairs. "We caught this gringo crossing your land. We were waiting to begin punishment until you arrived."

"Proceed with the punishment!" he proclaimed. The patron wanted his guests to see how he treated every gringo from the Arizona Territory who was found on the rancho.

Don Ramon's segundo, Pablo Mendoza, stepped forward

with a large whip in his hand. Mendoza was a short fat man with menacing beady eyes, a scraggly beard, and virtually no neck. His short vest and pants were soiled and dirty, and his sombrero was frayed and ragged on one edge. Mendoza wore two belts of rifle cartridges that intersected across his huge stomach.

He smiled, revealing rotting teeth as he swung the whip, lashing the cowboy across the back. The man from the Arizona Territory cried out.

Ricardo was half asleep from being on a horse throughout the night, but the crack of the whip jolted him back into reality and he focused on the cowboy for the first time, recognizing him.

"Wait!" he said loudly. "I know that man. His name is Bob Hastings, and he has a small spread near my grandmother's ranch."

"He's a gringo. I hate gringos!" the don proclaimed, eyes glistening with excitement.

"Stop whipping him! He's a friend of mine," Ricardo yelled.

The whip lashed across Hastings' back a second time, and the cowboy yelled loudly.

"I said stop!" Montoya ordered.

Don Ramon smiled. "This is my ranch, and don't you forget it!"

Ricardo grabbed the fat rancher by his pony tail and the seat of his pants and pulled him over to the top of the railing, causing the hacienda owner to scream.

"Tell him to bring Hastings up here, or by God, I'll throw you off the balcony," Ricardo warned.

"Pablo! Bring him up here! Bring him up!" the terrified rancho owner yelled.

Soto reached for a knife under his vest just as Rafael shoved the barrel of his revolver into Soto's side. "Drop your knife on the floor, or I'll blow a hole through you," Rafael growled. Soto flashed him a look of pure hatred. Rafael cocked his revolver, and the Spaniard dropped his knife.

For the first time, Christina realized how deadly the Mexican frontier was. She saw around her dangerous men with totally different views of right and wrong. Her uncle believing his position in life as a don entitled him to total control, while Ricardo believed in justice, the end justifying the means.

The fat Mexican used a knife to cut the rope from Bob Hastings' arms. He pushed the Arizona Territory rancher to the stairs, and they climbed to the balcony. When the two men reached the top of the stairs, Aragon pointed at Ricardo. "Kill him!" the patron yelled.

His segundo lunged at Ricardo, knife in hand. Montoya grabbed his arm and smashed his fist into Mendoza's face. The knife dropped to the floor and the two men whirled around and crashed into the wrought iron railing that encircled the upstairs balcony. Mendoza tried to push Ricardo over the side, but Montoya swung the fat Mexican in a circle and hit him in the face again. The force of the blow knocked Mendoza hard against the railing. The metal fence snapped and Mendoza toppled into space. When he smashed into the ground, he lay in a twisted, misshapen position on the hard packed earth, unable to move, crying out for help.

Ricardo grabbed Don Ramon by the front of his shirt. "Do exactly what I tell you, or so help me, I'll throw you over the side!"

"Yes! Yes! Anything!" he pleaded, his face covered in sweat. "Don't hurt me!"

"Tell your men to saddle four horses and bring three more as spares. You, Bob Hastings, Rafael, and I are all leaving. Once we are far enough away from the rancho, I will release you and you can ride back here."

"But there might be Apaches out there!" the frightened don cried out.

Ricardo, short of sleep and patience, pushed the don up against the metal railing. "Do it or I'll throw you off the balcony," he growled.

Terrified, Aragon yelled instructions to his men.

Aunt Olivia could take no more. She sat down with a thud and fainted. Christina bent over her. "Someone please help her" she pleaded.

"Soto. Pick her up and take her inside," Ricardo ordered.

"I'm not a servant," Miguel said in a disgusted voice.

Ricardo grabbed him by the front of his shirt. Montoya's eyes narrowed, and a look of fury came over his face. "Listen, you bastard. Do what I tell you."

Rafael knew his brother was at the end of his patience. "He's in no mood to play games, Soto. Get busy."

Soto grabbed Aunt Olivia under the arms and tried to lift her, but the fat woman was more than he could carry. He struggled as he pulled her along the floor. "Use a little more muscle," a grinning Rafael recommended.

Christina did not see humor in the situation. "For God's sake, someone help him," she said loudly.

Rafael bent over and grabbed Olivia's feet. Together they carried her inside and laid her on a couch. "Now, get back outside," Rafael told Soto.

Soto's face showed pure loathing. He had been ordered around, treated like a servant, and yelled at. His station in life had always been at the very top of the Spanish hierarchy, and now he had been degraded by men from a peon heritage. Miguel lunged at Rafael, who smashed him in the face. Soto hit the floor and slowly climbed back on his feet, shaking his head from side to side.

Rafael grabbed him by the front of his jacket and slapped him hard across the face. "Don't do that again. I'm losing my patience."

***

The Spaniard stumbled back out onto the balcony. Ricardo was intently watching as the vaqueros saddled the horses and brought three extra horses up to the assembled group. The injured segundo had been taken away.

"Watch Soto and Aragon. I want to speak to Christina," he said quietly to his brother.

Rafael nodded in agreement. Ricardo entered the second floor room. Christina had put a damp wash cloth across her aunt's forehead. Ricardo walked over to Aunt Olivia and examined her.

"She'll be all right. She just fainted," he said.

Christina's bright blue eyes fixed on Ricardo's face.

"I'm going to marry Miguel anyway. There's probably some truth to what you say, but I can not betray my family."

This was the low point of a rotten day for Ricardo. He decided that tact and diplomacy were out of the question. "You love me, and I love you. We were meant to be together. You are throwing away what could be a wonderful life for the two of us."

"I can't—"

"Let me finish! You're going to find out what a faithless, lying, totally corrupt man he is. But you will already be married. You are Catholic, so there is no chance for a divorce. You are sentencing yourself to a miserable life. And for what?

112

Money!" Ricardo emphasized.

Tears filled her eyes, and she began to shake.

Ricardo stepped forward and put his hands on her shoulders.

"Don't, please!" she told him, and stepped backwards.

He pulled her to him anyway and held her while she cried. Minutes later he exited the room, and the four men descended the stairs to where the horses were waiting.

"Tell them that no one is to follow us, and this means Soto in particular. Tell them that your life depends on it," Montoya said in a hard voice.

Don Ramon looked into Ricardo's eyes and knew that he meant it. He gave the prescribed orders to his men, and the group mounted their horses and rode east. Rafael broke off from the group and circled around to make sure that they were not being followed. After about five miles, the three men halted and waited for Rafael to reappear. When he rode up and reported that no one had left the rancho, Ricardo turned to Don Ramon. "You are free to go. If anyone follows us, I'll go back to your rancho and kill you. Is that clear?"

"Yes. Yes!" the wide-eyed don said in a frightened voice.

"Well, what are you waiting for?" a smiling Rafael asked.

Aragon turned his horse around and galloped away.

Bob Hastings thanked the brothers for saving him. "I think I would be a dead man if you hadn't shown up."

"How's the back?" Rafael asked.

"I've had a lot worse."

Hastings explained that he had rounded up twelve head of cattle and was driving them north to the border when the vaqueros jumped him. "The cattle didn't have any brands on them, and I didn't realize I was on someone's private land. I was just taking them back to Arizona to make a little extra money for the family."

"When we get back, I'll see that grandmother gives you a dozen cows to make up for this."

"Well, I sure appreciate that," said Hastings. "Times are tough for a small rancher."

"Where are we headed?" Rafael asked.

"I want to follow the tracks of the Apache band and see where they're going," Ricardo replied.

The three men headed east and crossed the tracks of the Apaches about mid-afternoon. They followed at a distance where they would not be discovered, stopping occasionally to eat and rest the horses. Then the Indians' trail turned southeast. The brothers looks at the tracks and then at each other.

"I know where they're headed, the rancho owned by Don Carlos Bustamante," Ricardo growled.

Rafael nodded his head in agreement.

CHAPTER 13

Ricardo looked over at Bob Hastings while they were resting their horses. "Bob, if you don't mind, I'd like you to ride up to our ranch and tell Victoria that Rafael and I will be along as soon as we warn the people on the Bustamante rancho about the Apache threat."

Hastings saw through the polite ruse that Montoya had put forth. "You know I'm pretty good with a rifle," he pointed out. "I owe you for saving my life."

"You're a family man, Bob. There's no sense in your wife becoming a widow with three kids." Ricardo's method of communication was direct and straight forward, and Hastings winced.

"I need someone to tell her where we are and what's going on. I'd sure appreciate it, Bob, if you would carry the message to her."

"All right, Ricardo. I can't turn you down."

The brothers watched the young rancher ride away. "You were pretty smooth," Rafael commented.

"He's a family man, and he shouldn't get himself killed just because he feels obligated."

"Don't try and pull that on me," Rafael said.

They kept well away from the Apache camp as they made a circle around the hostiles' bivouac. The brothers tied their horses and moved as close as they could to the Apaches. There were three small fires, and the Apaches moved around them as they began to eat. Rafael counted thirty-seven braves. Ricardo thought the number was thirty-eight. They quietly returned to their horses, mounted, and rode to the Bustamante hacienda.

***

The Apaches were led by Red Lance, Sky Walker's son. He had scouted the Bustamante rancho and determined that it was an easy mark. The original plan was to wait for Chatto, another Apache leader, to bring his followers to join the raid, but Red Lance was impatient. He wanted to raid, rape, and kill now, and not wait longer. The smaller rancho was to be a prelude to a larger target, Don Ramon Aragon's hacienda, a much bigger assimilation of houses and mining facilities. The second raid would provide a larger haul of provisions, guns, women, and gold. Red Lance moved from campfire to campfire, telling his men how simple the Bustamante raid would be.

Taza, a tall brave with a long face, had been Chatto's messenger. He confronted Red Lance about the change of plans. "Why do you not want to wait for Chatto?"

Red Lance did not like having his orders questioned. "It is my decision. We will raid the small rancho first," he said gruffly.

"A larger number of braves makes an attack much easier," Taza pointed out.

"This is not your decision. You can stay here if you like. But my band will attack at sunrise."

Taza was not impressed by Red Lance's bravado. "I will

116

wait here until Chatto arrives with our group. Those were my orders."

"Then do as you please," said Red Lance. He turned and walked away.

***

The Montoya brothers were able to ride up to the Bustamante house without anyone challenging them. "Where the hell are the lookouts?" Rafael asked. The brothers knocked on the front door, and a maid opened it slightly.

"We are Rafael and Ricardo Montoya to see Don Carlos," said Ricardo.

She recognized Ricardo, opened the door, and smiled. "He will be happy to see you," she stated, and hurried away.

"Not when he hears what we have to tell him," Rafael noted.

A sleepy-eyed Don Carlos Bustamante came rushing up to Ricardo and grasped his hand. "It's so good to see you!" he exclaimed. "Don Carlos, I think you met my brother, Rafael, before." The two men shook hands. "I'm afraid I bring bad news. There's a large Apache band a couple of miles from here, and I think they are going to attack your hacienda, probably in the early morning."

"Oh, no! We haven't had a raid here in a long time. Are there many?" he asked in a worried voice.

"Yes. Close to forty braves from what we could see."

The don's face turned white.

"How many vaqueros do you have who can shoot?" Rafael asked.

The worried don thought for a moment. "Nine," he said quietly. "The rest are away on a roundup. Hopefully, the peons you taught to shoot will have remembered some things from your instruction."

"Gather all of the men, women, and children here in the hacienda. Tell them to bring every weapon they can find," Ricardo emphasized.

The rotund don hurried away. He issued orders to his servants, and they ran to the surrounding adobe houses. Within an hour, all of the peons, vaqueros, and their families were assembled in a square courtyard in the center of the hacienda. Women and children were crying, and men had worried looks. Ten vaqueros were away on the roundup.

Ricardo and Rafael walked around the parapet at the top of the walls surrounding the hacienda. Various rooms in the hacienda had gun slits from which the Mexicans could fire out. The walls were two feet thick, and the only entrances and exits were two sets of double doors on the north and south sides of the square building.

"What do you think?" Ricardo asked his brother.

"You and I should be at each end on the parapets near the doors. It's the only way they can get in unless they have ladders. We should be able to pick them off before they mount a full scale attack," Rafael replied.

The brothers inspected the peons' rifles and pistols, and placed the Mexican farmers at various gun slits in the ground floor rooms. The vaqueros would be on top of the building behind the parapet walls with the Montoya brothers.

Don Carlos had dressed in his finest clothing. A blue vest with heavy embroidery and gold buttons complimented his tight-fitting trousers that had gold buckles lining each leg. His dark sombrero was similarly enhanced with embroidery and gold ribbon. The don had recovered his composure and was angry that Apaches were about to attack. If he was about to meet his maker, he wanted to go out in style. "I want to kill those bastards!" he exclaimed.

"You will get your chance, Don Carlos," Rafael promised him.

The families bedded down in the hacienda rooms that were in an L-shape on the inside of the adobe walls. Most of the women and children fell asleep on straw mattresses or blankets. Many of the peons and vaqueros tried unsuccessfully to sleep, but were too worried about their families. Vaqueros took Rafael and Ricardo's places above while the brothers tried to get a little sleep. About four in the morning, the Montoyas arose and climbed stairs to the top of the walls.

***

Thirty minutes later the Apaches entered the outskirts of the rancho and began sacking the adobe houses, finding no one. As light began to creep over the horizon, they had been in all of the adobe homes and found them empty.

"They knew we were coming," a brave said to Red Lance.

"It makes no difference. We found ladders here, so we can use them to get over the walls."

***

An unusual quiet prevailed, punctuated only by a bird calling to its mate. Rafael was first to spot the Apaches moving from house to house, and he turned and motioned to his brother that the Apaches were coming. Below, a vaquero moved from one firing slit to another to alert the peons.

"Let's begin," Ricardo stated. He took aim with his rifle and fired. A brave jumped in the air and fell to the ground, his body contorting, feet thrashing in the dirt. Rafael took his first shot and a brave fell backwards, a bullet through the chest.

Red Lance eagerly urged his men forward, and the Apaches shattering the quiet with yells and cries as they rushed the walls with ladders on two sides. The Montoya brothers moved along the walkways on the inside of the parapet walls, continually firing their repeating rifles. Inside the rooms, peons were shooting at the braves through gun slits but failed to hit any. Women and children began to scream and wail.

Inside one of the rooms, a peon looking through the gun slit was shot in the face and fell dead. Rafael moved to where an outside ladder was up against the wall, Apaches quickly scaling the ladder, and fired directly into the face of the first brave climbing to the top. The Apache screamed and fell, knocking the brave below him off the ladder. Rafael emptied his revolver into the oncoming Apaches as they neared the top, wounding four more and slowing the advance upward. He quickly reloaded his revolver from the bandoleer across his chest.

A brave reached the top of the ladder and Rafael hammered him across the face with his rifle butt, causing the Apache to do a backward somersault off the ladder. The next brave fired his revolver at Rafael and the bullet went through his shoulder without breaking bones. Montoya felt the pain but kept striking the braves, smashing them over the head as they reached the top of the ladder. Apaches reached the gun slits and began firing through at the Mexican faces on the other side. Two more peons were killed.

***

Ricardo was similarly engaged in the firefight. As one Apache would reach the top, Ricardo would pick him off, using his revolver. Don Carlos was standing in the courtyard, directing his fire at the Apaches as they appeared.

Two of the Indians dropped into the courtyard, wounded, and were killed by the waiting Mexicans. Two more braves appeared at the top of the ladder, and Ricardo shot one. His revolver empty, he began swinging his rifle at the Apaches as they came up the ladder and over the wall. A brave slashed at Ricardo with his knife, cutting him across the chest. He clubbed two more Apaches and they fell into the courtyard. A brave vaulted over the top of the wall and into the melee below. The Apache's first shot knocked a vaquero down in front of Don Carlos, and the rancher put a bullet between the Apache's eyes.

***

Red Lance continually urged his men upward until a brave grabbed him by the shoulder. "We've lost more than half of our men. Do you want to kill all of us?"

A feeling of dismay suddenly struck Red Lance. He remembered Sky Walker's admonition about there being no one to replace fallen warriors. He called his men back, and the remaining nineteen Apaches quickly moved out of rifle range. The attack had been a dismal failure due to poor planning, terrible strategy, and an overwhelming desire to kill at all costs. The braves trashed the small adobe buildings, set fires where they could, and then retreated back to their camp with as much food and supplies as they could carry, along with their wounded companions.

***

Inside the compound, there was a feeling of euphoria as the Mexicans realized they had survived. They put bullets through the wounded Apaches' heads. Seventeen Apaches were dead, five vaqueros and peons had perished, but the Mexicans had prevailed.

Don Carlos walked up to Ricardo, put his arms around the tall man, and gave him a mighty hug, not paying attention to Montoya's wound, carried away with delight. Ricardo groaned, feeling the wound for the first time.

"We would all be dead if it were not for you!" he happily cried out. "That's the third time you have saved my life."

Rafael came down off the parapet. He was grimacing with pain from the shoulder wound, and when he sat down he was attended to by two Mexican women who wrapped his shoulder wound. "Are either one of you women single?" he asked, face distorted but smiling.

"I am," a pretty, dark haired girl stated.

"You'll have to give me special attention," said Rafael.

While Ricardo's wound was being attended to, Don Carlos and two of his vaqueros walked around the perimeter of the hacienda, checking to see if any of the braves were still alive. None were. As they retreated, the Apaches had taken their wounded with them. The Mexicans moved as a unit, putting out fires and assessing the damage.

For the next two days, Ricardo was too sore to participate as Don Carlos and his men began rebuilding some of the facilities. Rafael had found a very attentive woman to see to his needs, and was on his way to a speedy recovery. Don Carlos sent a messenger to Hermosillo, and twelve vaqueros arrived at the rancho to protect the families until his cowboys returned from the roundup.

Montoya told Bustamante that he had to leave, much to the don's dismay. "I need to try and find out where those Apaches will strike again," he explained. "There is a half-Apache woman at the new rancho we have purchased. She may know."

"I understand, but you are not in shape to ride far," said Bustamante.

"The knife cut is painful but not serious. My brother needs a few more days of rest. I'll be back to get him," Montoya stated.

Rafael told his brother not to hurry, he was receiving excellent care. Ricardo made the ride to his new rancho, Vista

Bonita, in a day and a half. Chata's hugely fat husband was asleep in the same chair he was in when Ricardo last saw him.

She emerged from the house and fixed her gaze on Montoya. Chata looked more Mexican than Apache, hair pulled back in braids, and wearing a simple, beige cotton dress. Around her waist was a silver studded belt, beaded moccasins completing the outfit.

"Hello, Chata."

She nodded in response and noted that he had been wounded, but never took her eyes off his face. Her stoic countenance was neither hostile nor friendly, and her facial expression never changed.

"Could I trouble you for something to eat?"

"Come inside. Do you want me to change the dressing on your wound?"

He nodded yes. She changed the bandage but never said a word. Ricardo explained about the raid at Don Carlos Bustamante's rancho. As he ate, he attempted to make conversation but to no avail. *I guess I will have to be direct*, he surmised.

"Chata, I know you are in contact with Sky Walker on a regular basis, and I'm fine with that. In fact, I like the idea. By now, you know we have reached an agreement whereby men from this rancho will not bother his band in the mountains. And, he will not raid Vista Bonita, which is the new name for this rancho."

She looked at him but said nothing.

"I would appreciate it if you would talk to me. I am not your enemy," Ricardo emphasized.

"What is it you want to know?" she said after a few moments.

"My brother, Rafael, also was wounded in the fight.

You've met him. When he is well enough to travel, he will return here to be the don. Did you know about the attack at the Bustamante rancho?"

She hesitated, not knowing how much she should tell him. "I know about it."

"Did any of the braves come from Sky Walker's band?"

"No, but there's a great deal of unrest. Men from various groups of Apaches—Chiricahuas, Mescaleros, and some from the San Carlos Reservation—are banding together to raid in Mexico."

Ricardo chewed his food and thought for a moment. "Are there more braves headed here?"

"Yes."

"Do you know who will lead them?"

"There are two leaders who may combine their forces. One is Red Lance, who is Sky Walker's son. The other is Chatto, a Mescalero from the eastern Arizona border country."

"How soon before they might combine forces?"

She thought for a moment. "In a few days."

"I appreciate you being honest with me."

"Sky Walker said you are a fair man."

"You and your husband will always be welcome here as I have told you before. I would like you to stay. I want to be able to communicate with Sky Walker through you, if you are agreeable."

Sky Walker had asked her to watch what happened and report to him on a regular basis. Now, Ricardo was asking her to do the same thing. "I agree," she said.

"I have one more question," Montoya said.

Her dark eyes never left his face. "What is it?"

"When the two bands get together, where will they go?"

Chata looked away for the first time, thinking about her

obligation to her own people versus feeding information to Montoya. "I don't know."

"Take a guess," he said in a quiet voice, continuing to chew his food.

Her gaze returned to Ricardo's face. "There's a large rancho several days west of here where they mine gold and silver. It could be one of the targets, or it might not. That's all I know."

Ricardo coughed as he choked on his food. His eyes widened as the realization about the Apaches' destination came into focus. Chata was referring to Don Ramon Aragon's hacienda.

CHAPTER 14

Chatto was heavy set through the shoulders and waist, and had an almost square, block-shaped head, deeply lined across the forehead, cheeks, and broad chin. Chatto's eyes were dark slits, and his expression stoic. He was a medicine man or shaman in the Mescalero tribe, not a chief, but braves followed him because of his fighting exploits. He was fearless, made good tactical decisions, and had taken more scalps than any man in his clan. He rode into the campsite where Red Lance awaited him, and was disgusted by what he saw. Chatto sat on his horse and looked at a defeated group of braves, several of them wounded. His messenger, Taza, approached the shaman.

"What happened?" he asked gruffly.

"Red Lance decided to attack a hacienda to the east of here. The Mexicans must have seen his braves coming, and were waiting in a heavily fortified rancho where they could shoot down on his men as they tried to climb the walls. He lost half of his braves. This is all that's left."

"Was he successful?"

"No. They came away without a single scalp, one of his

men is dying, and three are not fit for travel. Only ten of his fighting braves remain ready. Some left after the defeat, no longer wanting to follow him," Taza noted.

"Send him over to me," Chatto stated. He turned and motioned for the braves behind him to dismount. The leaders had met only once before when it was decided they would strike Don Ramon Aragon's cattle ranch and mining operation. Some of the peons in the mine had Apache blood, and word had traveled back to the reservation about large quantities of gold nuggets being pulled from the mine.

Red Lance approached Chatto. "Are your remaining men ready to travel?" Chatto asked. The medicine man completely ignored the devastating battle that had destroyed more than half of Red Lance's men, believing he had suffered humiliation enough.

Red Lance had a sullen expression on his face, but felt some hope that he might rise above the debacle. "Yes. There are ten braves ready to go."

"With your ten braves and my sixty, we should still have enough to raid the rancho where they mine the gold. With gold we can do much for our people."

"And much for ourselves. We can buy the finest horses, guns, and women," Red Lance exclaimed.

Chatto purposely stayed on his horse, and Red Lance had to look up to talk to him. "I will give you orders to pass on to your braves. You and your men will do exactly as I say. Is that clear?" Chatto declared.

Anger welled up in Red Lance. It showed in his face and eyes in particular, but he said nothing.

"If you don't want to follow my orders, then we will leave now and you can do whatever you want," said Chatto.

The thought of a great victory ahead was enough to make

Red Lance swallow his pride. "We will do as you say."

"Your wounded men will have to stay here. We can not take them with us."

"But the Mexicans may find them. It's almost a sure death sentence!" Red Lance pointed out.

"That is not my problem," Chatto said sternly as he stared at the younger warrior.

Red Lance knew from Chatto's stoic look and unrelenting demeanor that further argument was useless. He shook his head in agreement. "All right."

***

The combined forces rode away the following morning, leaving food and water for four wounded braves. Don Carlos Bustamante's men began scouting the area to determine if Indians remained, and one of the scouts discovered the wounded braves. The don led ten vaqueros, who attacked the Apaches just before dark and killed all four. Don Carlos had shed his mild manner and become a man bent on revenge for the injustice sustained by his people.

***

Ricardo rode fast for two days, switching from one horse to another and intersecting with the Apaches' tracks several miles from Aragon's rancho and mining headquarters. The two-story, fortress-like building was in the center of rings of smaller adobe houses extending out for a quarter of a mile. A hard packed dirt road led into the foothills, and ended at the mine entrance nearly a mile away. Mining equipment and processing facilities were located beside a fast moving creek coming down from the mountains beside the mine entrance. The don had a body guard of twenty men, and another ten vaqueros did the normal ranching activities involving horses and cattle. Defense of the hacienda fell to thirty men.

Approximately one hundred Mexicans, mostly miners, women, and children, rounded out the rancho's population.

Using binoculars, Ricardo watched the Apaches from a mountainside vantage point as they carefully examined their target.

***

"If we attack the workers on their way to the mine entrance, it would alert the families around the hacienda and they would group at the main ranch house," Taza observed, looking at Chatto inquiringly.

The medicine man nodded in agreement. "We'll have our men move quietly throughout the community and attack the rancho and adobe homes simultaneously. Let's watch their activities tomorrow and attack the following morning before day break. Prisoners will tell us where the gold is stored," Chatto replied.

Montoya and the Apache leaders were about sixty yards apart on the mountainside as they contemplated their options. Ricardo stayed hidden among the boulders but occasionally would glance at Chatto's location.

The medicine man felt someone was watching, but couldn't see a person or movement. "Do you see anyone?" he asked Taza.

Taza scanned the rocky hillsides around their position. "No, I don't think anyone has seen us," he responded. Chatto finally shrugged it off as being overly cautious, and the Apaches departed to join their band.

***

Montoya was able to evade sentinels put out at various locations around the compound, and approached the main house after dark. He moved silently up the stairs to where a guard was smoking and looking out toward the mine. Ricardo

129

jabbed his revolver barrel into the vaquero's back, took the man's rifle and revolver, and laid them on the wooden floor.

"Open the door. We're going in," he said quietly.

Seated around the dining room table were Christina, Aunt Olivia, Ramon Aragon, and Miguel Soto. Light radiated from Christina's light pink silk dress, and her dark hair fell around her shoulders, accenting her beautiful facial features.

Ricardo entered the room and pushed the vaquero to one side. The assembled people had astonished looks on their faces as they stared at Montoya. Food dropped from Aunt Olivia's open mouth. Don Ramon's eyes were wide and bulging. Soto's face displayed loathing. Christina sat back in her chair, flabbergasted. Montoya put his revolver back in its holster as he walked slowly up to the table.

"I'm not here to harm anyone. I'm here to warn you!"

"How dare you enter my house like this?" Don Ramon demanded.

"Shut up and listen!" Ricardo commanded. "Don Carlos Bustamante's hacienda was attacked by about forty Apaches. My brother and I helped the vaqueros fight them off, and we killed nearly half of them. The remaining braves joined another large group of hostiles yesterday. Out in the mountain foothills near your mine are about seventy Apaches waiting to attack tomorrow."

Aunt Olivia's face turned white, and she was on the verge of fainting again. Don Ramon's face turned bright red.

"Pepe!" he yelled at the vaquero standing against the wall. "Tell the body guards and vaqueros we leave within the hour. Get the coach ready to go."

"Wait a minute!" Ricardo roared. "You can't leave all those women and children to die. What the hell's wrong with you?"

"My safety is first and foremost. Olivia and Christina must be protected," he sputtered.

"We can form a good defense if we move everyone up to the mine tonight. We can confront the Apaches with gunfire from within the mine and drive them away," Ricardo emphasized.

"We are not taking any chances. We are leaving tonight. Peons can always be replaced," the don growled.

***

That statement struck Christina like a blow to the body. She was a conflicted woman who suddenly realized that basic principles of honor, integrity, and character would not be exercised when it came to the lower classes. At her father's rancho in Spain, servants and workers were treated almost like family.

She glanced at Ricardo and saw a man whose code of conduct extended to all men and women. He was honest, straight forward, and did what he thought was proper in the name of justice, even though his methods were severe, she reasoned. Then she turned her head towards her uncle. Here was a devious, disrespectful man, an unabashed coward with few morals.

"At least give your body guards and vaqueros the choice of staying and fighting or going with you," Ricardo stated.

"I'll need every one of them for protection," the don said in a loud voice.

"The Apaches will not attack you at night. They will try to surprise the peons tomorrow morning. It's the way they function," Ricardo explained.

Christina had had enough. "Stop!" she said loudly. She got up from the table and moved quickly until she was looking down at her uncle. All eyes were on her. "Uncle, you will give the men the choice or I will not marry Miguel Soto. And I will see to it that you do not get any money from my father," she stated in an angry voice. Her bright blue eyes blazed as she stared at Don Ramon.

Aragon believed her and quickly reassessed his position. "Are you sure the Apaches won't attack the coach as we leave?" he asked Ricardo.

"I'm positive. They want to use the element of surprise early tomorrow," Ricardo said. "They don't like fighting in the dark."

"Pepe, assemble the men!" the don shouted.

Within fifteen minutes, the fighting men on the rancho were grouped together near the hacienda. Aragon and Montoya walked down the stairs and stood in front of the men.

"Now listen up," Montoya commanded. "There is a large group of Apaches, probably sixty or more, waiting to strike the peons as they go to the mine tomorrow morning. Don Ramon and his guests are leaving tonight for Hermosillo. Those of you who want to stay and fight with me can do so. The rest of you can go with Don Ramon."

The men began talking loudly among themselves. "What chance do we have of surviving?" one bodyguard called out.

"A good chance. We will take everyone to the mine tonight; men, women and children. When the attack comes tomorrow, we will defend the mine entrance. We'll fight them off and we'll win!" Ricardo exclaimed in a loud voice.

"If we stay, a lot of us will die," a vaquero stressed.

"If you don't stay and fight, all of the women and children will die. It's that simple," said Ricardo in a resounding voice.

"Those of you who want to go with me, saddle your horses," Don Ramon ordered.

Again the men began talking among themselves, and then individuals started breaking away from the group to saddle up. Of the twenty bodyguards, only five remained behind. Eight of the ten vaqueros stayed, giving Ricardo a total of thirteen fighting men. All of those who chose to stay had wives and children or other relatives at the rancho.

Miguel Soto, Aunt Olivia, and Christina came down the stairs and prepared to enter the coach.

"I hope they kill you, you son of a bitch," Soto growled as he got into the coach.

Christina stopped walking and closed her eyes for a moment. Reality set in and her love for Ricardo would no longer allow her to pretend otherwise. *I can't go on with this charade*, she thought. *If I marry Miguel, I will be miserable my whole life.*

She turned, walked back to Ricardo, and looked into his eyes in the dim light. "Come for me when this is over," she whispered. "I love you."

Ricardo's emotions were in turmoil when he heard those words, and he wanted desperately to take her in his arms, the craving nearly overwhelming. "I'll find you no matter how long it takes," he replied. "I love you."

Christina smiled, turned, and hurried over to the coach. Five minutes later the coach pulled away with the group of armed men split equally in front and back of the carriage.

CHAPTER 15

It was another hour before more than one hundred men, women, and children were assembled. Women and babies were crying. Peons and vaqueros moved among the group trying to comfort the frightened people, but to no avail. Most women feared they had been condemned to death by the departure of Don Ramon and his bodyguards.

Ricardo took a deep breath. "Quiet down and listen to me!" he commanded. "We are going to make the mile walk to the mine as quickly and as quietly as possible. When we arrive at the mine, try to make yourselves comfortable. The fighting men and I will be at the entrance, and we'll fight them off and you will survive."

The procession began its trek along the dirt packed road, wide enough to accommodate wagons as they moved to and from the mine. The group was relatively quiet, with most babies sleeping in their mothers' arms. The first half mile took an hour with only moonlight to illuminate the line of frightened Mexicans.

***

As they neared the mine entrance an Apache lookout

heard them, quickly ran to the Indian camp, and awoke Chatto. Within minutes the medicine man gathered the Apaches and led the group towards the mine entrance.

The Mexicans began entering the mine as the Apaches arrived. With blood-curdling cries breaking the evening's silence, the Apaches fell upon the end of the procession as it passed into the mine. The night was filled with the roar of gunfire as Ricardo and the Mexicans standing near the entrance poured rifle and revolver fire into the massed Apaches running towards the entrance, using their tomahawks and rifles to kill stragglers. The deadly hail of Mexican bullets knocked down the front rank of Apaches, but the braves pressed forward, crazed by the desire to kill. Ten Mexican shooters used their rifles and revolvers at point blank range, every shot hitting an Apache, slowing down the charge.

Chatto yelled for his men to stop and take cover when he realized so many of his warriors were down and wounded. Indians moved to the sides of the road and took cover behind boulders. Firing ceased as quickly as it had begun.

I knew we were being watched, Chatto thought. *Whoever's leading them knows what he's doing.* Injured warriors were attended to, and the dead were covered with blankets. A wounded Mexican miner was tortured and revealed that the gold was stored in Don Ramon's headquarters building.

Sunrise revealed scattered bodies of Mexicans littering the area around the mine entrance. Chatto sent the majority of his braves into the community of adobe buildings and to the hacienda. They found an abundance of provisions in the peons' houses, and located one building that held mining supplies, including dynamite.

Don Ramon's home was ransacked and a large safe was discovered in an upstairs room. The Indians had no idea how to open or move it. Chatto had his men tie ropes to the safe and try to pull it through a doorway to the outside balcony, but the safe was larger than the doorway and the adobe walls were two feet thick. They soon lost interest and returned their attention to looting.

***

Ricardo was concerned about the Indians sealing off the entrance to the mine. "Is there another way out?" he asked one of the miners.

"There's a large air hole about a hundred yards into the mine," the peon told him.

Ricardo lit a torch and walked deep into the mine. Finding the location, he planted the torch in the wall and proceeded to climb up the rocky side of the air shaft until he was about ten feet from the top. There, the sides were smooth and he was unable to go higher. Climbing back down, he returned to where the mining equipment was stored and located a grappling iron, with three hooks protruding from the end of the tool. The grappling hook was used to pull sections loose from the walls of the mine when blasting was not an option. Ricardo tied a heavy rope to the end of the bar and procured a long pole.

Montoya enlisted two miners to help him and returned to the air hole that was about four feet in diameter at the top. He again climbed and reached the spot where he was unable to go higher. Ricardo had tied the pole to the end of the grappling iron and raised the apparatus above his head, lowered his arms, then heaved the pole upward. The grappling tool disappeared over the top of the air shaft just as it came loose from the pole. The pole shot backwards into the shaft, bouncing when it hit the rock floor.

Ricardo slowly pulled on the rope; the grappling hook

caught the rocks and held outside the shaft. He was breathing heavily, sweat pouring down his face into his eyes, as he slowly applied more pressure on the rope. The hook continued to hold. Montoya quickly climbed the rope, grabbed the top of the shaft, and lifted himself out just as the sun was coming over the horizon. He secured the grappling hook to keep it from coming loose, climbed back down into the mine, and returned to the main group of men, women, and children.

***

While looting the buildings, the Apaches found dynamite and blasting powder, and began preparing to carry it to the mine entrance. Chatto and Red Lance conferred and both were of the opinion that they should blow up the mine before they departed. One of the Apaches was half Mexican, had worked in a mine, and knew how to detonate dynamite.

"We can put it above the mine shaft and on the sides, and explode the dynamite by firing from long range," he told the leaders.

Taza wanted nothing to do with the idea. "I want to finish loading supplies on the pack horses. There's more than we can carry."

"Have you have lost your thirst for revenge? I want to kill them all!" Red Lance growled.

Taza turned and looked at Chatto for approval; the shaman nodded his head favorably, and Taza walked away, signaling his braves to follow him. The remaining Apaches roped together six large bundles of dynamite and carried them up the trail to the mine. The Indians began firing into the mine to create a diversion, while six braves carried the explosives to both sides of the entrance.

***

Ricardo and three vaqueros had climbed out of the mine

and were hidden on the rocky hillside above the mine. He realized what the Indians were about to do, and motioned for the Mexicans around him to stay hidden.

"At the count of three all of you fire at the dynamite being carried on the left," he said quietly, and pointed to where he wanted them to shoot. "I'll fire to the right side."

Ricardo took a deep breath. "One, two, three," he said to himself, and squeezed off a shot, his three companions firing simultaneously.

A thundering explosion blew away hillsides on both sides of the road, and the front of the mine disappeared. The blast was so powerful it threw rocks a hundred yards into the air, and filled the area with an enormous cloud of dust, dirt, and rocks. Even though Ricardo was behind a large boulder, the detonation threw him backwards. He landed on his back in a semi-conscious condition as the rocks rained down on top of him. Montoya began to gasp for air, his entire body covered with dirt and debris, making him unrecognizable. One of his companions was dead, while the other two were injured and began crying out. They, too, were covered in dirt and rocks, creating mummy-like figures with wide eyes. Montoya's mind and body were numb, and it took several minutes before he was able to focus on what had happened. He slowly sat up and began checking his arms and legs to determine if they still were functional.

***

The Indians carrying the explosives had disappeared. Those around them were hurled through the air and into the rocky hillsides. Red Lance had lost an arm and the side of his face. He thrashed around on the ground for a few moments before his life ended. Chatto was killed instantly.

Standing a quarter mile away, Taza was thrown off his

feet. He got up, stared at the huge cloud for a few moments, then turned and continued back to the rancho as rocks rained down on him. Taza sent two braves back to check for survivors, but they found none. He ordered the remaining eleven braves to finish loading provisions on pack horses, and they departed. *Never again will I have anything to do with dynamite*, Taza thought.

Several Mexicans climbed out through the air vent in the mine and administered aid to Ricardo and the two wounded vaqueros. More Mexicans soon exited through the vent and began digging away rocks and dirt from the sealed mine entrance. Others did the same on the inside. After two hours the entrance was opened and the families got their first view of the dynamite damage. What had been a road through rocky hillsides was now a mammoth crater. The road had disappeared, and so had large portions of the hills. Many of the families knelt and prayed. The remainder of the day was spent burying dead Apaches, or what was left of them.

***

By late afternoon Montoya had returned to normal, except for loud ringing in his ears, and called the people together.

"None of you should stay here unprotected. I will take all of you to Don Carlos Bustamante's rancho tomorrow. I'm sure he will allow you to live there as long as you want. My brother and I have purchased a rancho to the east. Those of you who want to live and work on my rancho are welcome, and no one will force you to leave," he told the gathered families.

There were excited exchanges of conversation among the peons and vaqueros, many smiling for the first time. A party of Mexicans searched for horses and mules that had fled following the explosion, and brought back nearly thirty before nightfall. Another search party found twelve more the following morning. The families packed their meager possessions in carts, women and children sitting on top of their belongings while men walked alongside. Twelve armed men on horseback encircled the long line of refugees as they advanced towards new lives.

The caravan had gone several miles when there were two more explosions behind them. Later a vaquero rode up to Ricardo and explained, "We just blew up the mine and his home. Don Ramon deserved it."

Montoya looked surprised, then began to laugh. "Don Ramon will think I did it," he told the messenger.

Travel was slow, with numerous stops along the way, and the caravan camped ten miles from the Bustamante rancho. A scout from the hacienda spotted the group, rode up, and dismounted.

"Ricardo, it is good to see you," an overjoyed vaquero said. Montoya explained what had occurred and who the refugees were, and the Mexican cowboy rode back to report to Don Carlos.

The following morning the procession moved slowly on to the Bustamante property. Ricardo's body ached, his face was covered with cuts and bruises, but the ringing in his ears was beginning to subside.

Don Carlos rode out to meet them and greeted Ricardo warmly. "I didn't expect to see you again so soon," he stated.

"Nor did I expect to be back here so quickly," Ricardo said. "How is my brother?"

This brought laughter from the don. "He has a way with women. The young ladies are taking turns attending to him. I don't think he will ever want to leave."

Ricardo grinned. "That sounds like Rafael." Montoya explained in detail what had happened over the past two days.

"I believe you, of course, but it's difficult to think that anyone would abandon people on his rancho to be butchered by the Apaches," Bustamante replied.

"The vaqueros blew up his mine and hacienda as going away presents," a smiling Ricardo explained.

Both men began laughing. "I'd like to see his face when he finds out his rancho is a pile of rubble," said Bustamante. Don Carlos turned in his saddle and looked back at the long line of refugees. "I can't take them all," Don Carlos lamented. "Our crops have been harvested, and there just wouldn't be enough food to go around until next season."

"I've invited them all to come and live on the rancho that Rafael and I have purchased. I'll ship the necessary foods to the rancho from the Arizona Territory."

Bustamante smiled. "My guess is that all of them will follow you."

"I hope they will. It would give Rafael and me the start of a good work force to rebuild that rancho and all of the surrounding buildings."

"How many people are in back of us?" the don asked.

"The number's about one hundred and ten men, women, and children," Ricardo responded. "More kept joining us as we traveled here. I don't know where some of them came from."

When the column reached the rancho, the ever-jovial Rafael quickly walked out to greet them. "Brother! I understand I missed all of the fun." Ricardo dismounted and the brothers embraced, Rafael staring at his brother's face. "What the hell happened to you?" he asked.

Bustamante's men led the procession to a large, open field behind the hacienda where they would camp for the night. At dinner, Ricardo took his time and explained in detail what had happened since the last time the three men were together. Rafael and the don had incredulous expressions on their faces.

"No one will believe this story about blowing up the Apaches," Rafael said, shaking his head from side to side.

"The strange thing is, if Don Ramon and his men had stayed to fight, the explosion wouldn't have taken place," Ricardo pointed out.

"And now he's a man without a rancho and mine," Rafael said jokingly.

After dinner, the three men walked to the field where the families were bedded down. One of the vaqueros approached them.

"May I have a word with you?" he asked the three dons.

"Of course," said Don Carlos.

"Two of the families would like to stay at your rancho, Don Carlos. They have relatives living here."

"They are welcome. Tell them to make arrangements with the families. I will provide food and shelter," Bustamante said.

The vaquero turned to Ricardo.

"The rest of the families would like to join you on your new rancho."

Ricardo smiled. "That's wonderful news. Tell them they are all welcome, and they will be protected."

The three men returned to the hacienda and sat on the porch drinking brandy. Rafael began laughing. "Can you visualize the look on Don Ramon's face when he sees his hacienda in rubble and his mine blown to pieces? He'll damn near have a heart attack."

They laughed and joked the way comrades and good friends enjoy each other's company. Don Carlos brought the conversation back to Don Ramon Aragon. "He probably will bring the army with him in order to take back control of his rancho. From what I understand, he pays the army commander in Hermosillo on a monthly basis to do his bidding. They will follow the trail of the fleeing peons and vaqueros, first here, and then to your new rancho. There's no telling what stories he will be telling the Mexican soldiers," Don Carlos stated.

"Let them come," said Rafael. "The peons and vaqueros are free men and women. They should be able to live wherever they want to live."

Bustamante frowned. "Many of the dons look upon them as being their own private property...you know that, Rafael. Don Diego Salazar was a good example. No one left his rancho."

"That's true," said Ricardo. "But circumstances are different here. We will be able to show that they were left to die and now want to begin new lives."

The men were momentarily quiet as they thought about the circumstances and consequences of what had transpired.

"Ricardo, he's a dangerous man. Be careful. Money and absolute power corrupt," Bustamante emphasized. "He's as dangerous as Salazar was."

Montoya sat back and lit a cigar. "We haven't talked about Maria. I hope she's happy. I fell in love with another woman, Christina Aragon, who is Don Ramon's niece. She's set to marry a man who will bring a great deal of money into the Aragon mining and cattle operations, Miguel Soto. She's ready to change her mind, and I intend to steal her away before the marriage."

Bustamante looked surprised. Rafael sat back in his chair and took a long sip of brandy, staring skyward. Ricardo told them about Christina and how she refused him, only to change her mind as Don Ramon and his men were leaving the rancho. Their eyes were riveted on Ricardo as he went through the whole scenario.

"If you break up that business arrangement between the Sotos and the Aragons, they will attempt to kill you," Bustamante declared.

"The wedding is set to take place in about a month and will be held in Hermosillo. She told me to come for her, and that is what I intend to do."

"You have picked the wrong woman at the wrong time," said a grinning Rafael. "But what the hell, you only live once."

CHAPTER 16

Rafael and the families of peons and vaqueros were getting settled on Rancho Vista Bonita while Ricardo rode north to visit his grandmother. He was to send food and other supplies to accommodate the families, and building materials with which to begin making renovations at the rancho.

Ricardo halted his horse at Paco Flores's stables at The Crossing. The stable doors were open and no animals were in the corral. Suddenly worried, he dismounted and quickly entered the office. The desk chair was laying on its side and papers were scattered around the floor. A feeling of dread came over Ricardo. He quickly walked up the street to the cantina, entered, and looked for the large Mexican woman who was the owner. Lupe, the proprietor, came out from the back room and a startled look crossed her face.

"What happened, and where is Paco Flores?" Ricardo asked in a loud voice.

"He was injured. He's in the back room. He...."

Montoya quickly walked past her and through a door to a room at the rear of the building. Paco Flores was lying on a small bed in the corner. His face was bruised, his left arm was bandaged, and the center of his body was wrapped in bandages. He managed a slight smile at the sight of his friend.

"Chameleon! It's good to see you," he said in a gravelly voice.

"What happened, Paco? How badly are you injured?"

"I think my arm is broken and some ribs, but I will be all right," he said, grimacing from the pain.

"Who did this to you?"

The man with the Santa Claus face was silent as he looked at the enraged Ricardo Montoya. Ricardo's eyes were mere slits and his jaws were shut tightly, giving him the look of a predator.

"The Baca brothers came into the stables, drunk. I tried to get them to leave, and it ended in a fight. I'm afraid they beat on me pretty good," he said quietly.

Ricardo stared at his friend as rage began building within. He had never known a kinder, nicer man, and Montoya's emotions were raw from recent events.

"Where is the best place for you to stay so you can be taken care of until I get a doctor down here from the Arizona Territory?" Ricardo asked.

Paco Flores thought for a moment. "The mercantile store has a couple of rooms in back that travelers stay in. One of those would do fine."

Flores did not object to being moved to better surroundings. "Lupe assisted me as much as she could, but she is alone and has to cook for a lot of people in the community. She is the only cook."

Montoya had a stretcher brought to the room, and Paco was transported to his new room. It contained a bed, bureau, two chairs, and art work on the walls. *This place needs a good cleaning, but it'll do,* Ricardo thought.

Montoya paid the store owner for a month's stay at double the going room rate. "When I return, if Paco says you have given him excellent service, I will double this amount as a bonus. See to it that all of his needs are met," he told a suddenly smiling owner.

"He will get the absolute best of care," the Mexican blurted out.

Ricardo returned to chat again with Lupe. They arrived at a daily rate for Paco's meals, and he paid her twice what she was asking for a month's worth of food. He told her that he would double that amount if Paco liked the food.

Lupe smiled and said Flores would receive the best food money could buy. Ricardo returned to Paco's room and found his friend smiling, enjoying the luxury of a real bed with pillows piled around him.

"Where do I find the Baca twins?"

Flores looked at his friend and could see smoldering anger just beneath the surface. "Please don't kill them, Ricardo. I don't want that on my conscience. I live here with these people, and they are my friends."

"I hear you," Montoya assured him. "But no men should be able to get away with this. You are a good person."

"Just don't kill them, please."

"All right. But I want to make sure this doesn't happen again."

Flores sighed and grimaced from the pain. "They could be in the bar or at their father's home at the end of this street."

Montoya walked back through the store and picked an ax handle out of a barrel. He flipped the owner a coin and began his walk to the bar. His bad temperament returned as he thought of what the two men had done to a kind man with no enemies in the world. Ricardo's feeling of hostility heightened as he entered the cantina.

The Baca brothers, as well as the other residents of the small community on the border, had watched as Montoya moved Flores to his new room. Jose and Pepe Baca were not impressed, and scowled at Ricardo. Now the bartender sensed trouble, and his hands dropped below the bar to where his shotgun was located. Montoya walked up to the man, glaring. "Put your hands on the bar. If they drop below it, you're a dead man," he warned the bartender. The bartender looked into Montoya's angry eyes, pulled his hands up quickly, and put them on the bar.

Ricardo's wild anger spilled over as he moved to where the brothers were standing at the far end of the bar. He thrust the ax handle into Jose's stomach, causing him to double over and cry out. Montoya then swung the ax handle and it cracked against Pepe's skull, sending him sliding down the bar. Returning his attention to Jose, he clubbed him across the head, knocking him to the floor. Montoya walked to the prone brother and smashed his pointed boot into the man's ribs, snapping several bones.

Pepe was holding on to the bar to keep from falling. "No please!" he cried out.

Montoya swung the ax handle in a low arch, and it crushed Pepes right shin just below the knee. Pepe began to shriek and cry out as he fell backwards onto the floor. To finish off his frenzy of anger, Ricardo buried his pointed boot into Pepe's ribs, with the same result.

Ricardo approached the bartender. "Where's their father?" he growled.

The bartender's eyes were wide and his mouth open as he stared at Montoya. "He's at his home at the end of the street."

Ricardo walked over to Pepe and grabbed the moaning

vaquero by the back of his shirt collar. He pulled him over to his brother, grabbed the second brother by his shirt, and dragged both men out into the street. The brothers were crying out like children as Montoya deposited them in the dirt.

"Just so we understand each other. If either one of you ever touches Paco Flores again, I'll find you. Then you'll answer to me and you'll be dead men!" Montoya put his foot on Pepe's chest and pushed, causing him to cry out.

"I understand! I understand!" he yelled.

Montoya then shifted his foot to Jose's leg.

"I promise! Nothing will happen to Paco ever again!" Jose shouted.

Townspeople had come to view what became known as "Ricardo's Revenge." More than a dozen Mexican men and women stood in silence as the scene unfolded before them. As Montoya moved up the street to find their father, the people slowly walked up to the notorious troublemakers.

There was only one house near the end of the street, and Montoya advanced at a rapid pace, anxious to be done with the retribution. A rifle bullet fired from the home whistled by Ricardo's head, and he ran to his right, jumped down into a drainage channel, and continued to run in a crouched position until he was alongside the small house. He jumped out of the arroyo and put his back against the side of the adobe structure. Looking in the small side window, he could see Marcos Baca aiming his rifle at the front door.

Ricardo took careful aim and fired, the bullet striking the rifle barrel just in front of Baca's hands, knocking it against the wall, momentarily stunning the old man. Running, Montoya circled the home to the front door, kicked it in, and jumped on Marcos as he was about to pick up his weapon. He wrestled the man to the ground and put his knee on Baca's chest.

"Why are you doing this to my family?" the frightened man yelled. "I don't even know you!"

"Your sons busted up Paco Flores pretty good. I just paid them back. If anybody touches Paco again, I'll come back and break every bone in your body. Is that clear?" Ricardo growled.

Marcos Baca looked into Montoya's eyes and saw anger and hostility that thoroughly frightened him. "Yes, I'll see that nothing happens to him again," Baca promised.

"I'll kill your boys if it happens again," Montoya warned. "Now get up, we're going to the stables."

The small Mexican shuffled down the middle of the street, then ran to his sons, who were being administered to by the townspeople.

"Oh, no!" he cried out. "Oh, boys!"

Ricardo was unrelenting, grabbed the father by his collar, and threw him forward towards the stables. He continued walking after Marcos Baca until the two of them reached the corral.

"You're to muck out the corral and the stables each day. You're going to live here, taking care of peoples' horses and collecting money. Resupply the hay when it's needed, and see that the animals are watered and rubbed down when they are brought to you. You'll continue to do this until Paco is well enough to return!"

Baca was frightened, terribly worried about his sons, and suddenly hated the man standing in front of him.

Ricardo continued. "The money you collect is to be given to the store owner. Is that clear?"

Marcos just stared at Montoya, anger welling up in him. Montoya slapped him hard across the face, knocking the man to the ground. "You've got no one to blame but yourself!"

Ricardo stated loudly. "What kind of low life bastards are you raising? Now, get busy!"

After Montoya departed, the father fell to his knees and put his hands over his eyes, tears rolling down his cheeks, and he kept repeating, "My boys! My boys!"

Montoya walked up the street to the store where Paco Flores was staying and went into Paco's room. "It's done. The two sons are feeling the same pain you felt. The father is taking care of the stables until you can return," said Ricardo, suddenly feeling exhausted.

"You have a lot of anger in you, Chameleon. You need time to rest and gather your thoughts. Everything is not black and white. All persons are not good or evil," said the kind stable owner.

Montoya thought about what Paco Flores said. "I do what I believe is right." Ricardo sat down in one of the chairs, red-eyed, tired, and breathing deeply as the two men looked at each other.

"I thank you for what you have done for me," Flores stated. "I don't mean to be critical of you. I admire your sense of justice and the way you have helped so many people. But you are not in the best frame of mind at the moment. You need some time to relax and reflect."

Montoya smiled at that statement and began to laugh. "Relax and reflect. I only wish I had the time. Let me tell you what has happened over the past month."

During the next half hour Ricardo reviewed everything that occurred, from the rape and murder on the Barringer ranch, to the fight with Apaches at Don Carlos Bustamante's hacienda, and finally to the battle with the Indians on Don Ramon Aragon's rancho. He even revealed his love for Christina Aragon. Flores plied him with inquisitive questions at various stages of the story.

"Don Carlos is a good man. Don Ramon is just the opposite, arrogant and cruel," Paco noted. "There's a family living here that used to live on Aragon's rancho. The stories they tell about him are difficult to believe. When he finds his rancho is a pile of rubble and all of his vaqueros and peons are gone, he will come after you to take them back."

"I'm in love with Christina Aragon, and I will be going back to Hermosillo to try to steal her away before the wedding. This will be the final insult that Aragon so richly deserves."

"That would ruin his plans for expanding his mining operations. Many politicians and army officers have stayed at his rancho. He uses money to buy influence, and he's very good at it," Paco pointed out.

Ricardo thought for a moment. "I'll deal with whatever happens."

"He will bring soldiers with him when he returns to his rancho. The Mexican government will be on his side," Flores stressed.

"I've thought about that, but right now I need to get food and supplies back to Vista Bonita so Rafael can begin feeding nearly a hundred and ten people and start the renovations to the hacienda and surrounding homes."

Flores nodded his head. "I understand."

"You should be safe. The Baca family knows what will happen to them if you are harmed in any way. What do those two brothers do when they are not drinking?"

"I've heard rumors that they are part of a gang of bandits operating out of Sasabe, just west of Nogales on the Arizona Territory side of the border. A man by the name of Vic Norris has a small ranch there, and I don't think he makes his money from ranching."

Montoya smiled. "You certainly gain a lot of information in your business."

"Everyone likes to talk, and men come and go from here all the time. A stable is a center of information," Paco said.

CHAPTER 16

Ricardo changed his clothing before he crossed the border, and once again was James Barringer. He stood at the top of the hill looking at the Barringer ranch house and the surrounding buildings, thinking the massive French colonial mansion looked as if it had been constructed for a king. A pillared veranda ran around the entire home, giving the house a regal look. Surrounding buildings stretched out for nearly half a mile in every direction. He could just make out the flowers in the rose garden that was Victoria's favorite place to stroll. Large orchards of fruit trees, plus vegetable and melon gardens, changed the rolling, grassy land into a patchwork of colors.

James wore a white bandana around his neck and had changed into a dark blue cotton shirt. His leather vest and matching slacks were light beige, and he wore a cream-colored Stetson. His palomino, Oro, nudged him on the shoulder, causing James to take a half step forward and smile. "Getting hungry are you, Oro? You can smell the oats and maybe the mares," James said as he stroked the palomino's muzzle.

Barringer rode his horse past numerous men and women

as he wound his way along the road past gardens, crops, and orchards. "Hello, Pepe," he yelled to one of the Mexicans. "Mike, it's good to see you," he told a horse wrangler as he stopped in front of the ranch headquarters.

Victoria was standing on the front porch dressed in a beautiful pastel purple dress with matching jewelry. "I was wondering when you'd return. Did everything go well?"

"Yes, as far as the citizenship papers and the purchase of the ranch."

"Come inside and let's talk," she said, smiling.

James gave his grandmother a hug and they walked into her office. He sat down opposite her desk, leaned back, and exhaled slowly. "It's been a month like none other that I can ever remember," he said.

Victoria scrutinized his face, peppered with small scrapes and cuts caused by the dynamite explosion. "What happened to your face?"

"I was too close to a dynamite blast. My ears are still ringing," he replied, and grinned. James took a few minutes to explain what had transpired when he returned to Mexico, glossing over dangerous encounters and battles.

Victoria wasn't fooled but didn't believe it was the right time to request details. "I was able to clear up the problems involving the shooting of those low lifes. You won't be charged with any crimes."

"That's good to know. How has Silk been performing?"

"Really well. He has a good command of men and is quickly learning how to run a large ranch. He's a good substitute for you when you're gone."

"I fell in love again," James said, giving his grandmother an embarrassed glance.

Victoria smiled, her curiosity aroused. "I hope this one

works out better than the last love affair."

"Me too." He began telling her details about his visit to Hermosillo and meeting Christina. James explained about the trip to Don Ramon Aragon's hacienda, and the episode involving Bob Hastings.

"Bob stopped by here and filled me in. Aragon must be as savage as Salazar was," she commented.

"They're two of a kind."

"I had Silk drive a small herd over to Hastings ranch. Bob was very appreciative," Victoria noted.

"I was going to ask you to do that," James replied.

A young woman entered the office. "Mrs. Barringer, Silk Mathews is here. Do you want him to wait?"

"No, show him in."

James and Silk greeted each other warmly and shook hands.

"It's great to have you back. I saw your horse in front," Mathews stated.

They chatted about the ranch for a few minutes.

"I just got back from the southwest section of the ranch. It looks like some or our cattle have been rustled. I was going to take Cap Ousterhout, head over there, and try to determine where they went," Mathews declared.

Victoria's eyes narrowed. "How many?"

"It's hard to tell. Probably five hundred or more. Cap will have a better idea."

Both Victoria and Silk looked at James. He thought for a moment.

"Each time I cross the border, I talk with Paco Flores, the owner of the stables at The Crossing. He hears everything, and told me that a band of outlaws is operating out of a small ranch near Sasabe, led by a man named Vic Norris."

"I'll get started in the morning," said Silk as he got up to leave.

"Wait. I have a story to tell you about the last month," James stated.

Mathews sat down again, and James reviewed the story about his sojourn to Hermosillo, the trip back to Don Ramon's ranch, and the subsequent fight that erupted over the beating Bob Hastings was being given. James continued with a description of the battle at Don Carlos Bustamante's hacienda, and the later fight at Aragon's rancho that ended with the dynamite explosion. Then he described the long procession of vaqueros, peons, and their families who had followed him to the new ranch.

"I want to take food and supplies back to the peons at the new rancho as quickly as possible, and there's another problem. Don Ramon will return and find his mine and rancho blown to pieces. I know he'll think I did it. He'll have a Mexican army escort because he has the money and the political clout," James stated. "Aragon will want those people taken back to his rancho, and I'll have to convince the army officers otherwise."

"But they have a constitution in Mexico," Victoria observed.

"In the far northern sections of Mexico the dons' rule, and the government backs them because they are the front line against the Apaches," James noted.

The three leaders at the Barringer ranch talked for another half hour. Victoria said she had ten wagons of supplies stored in one of the ranch warehouses ready to go.

"I want to put together one more wagon of food and farming tools for the Apaches that live in the mountains adjacent to Vista Bonita. Their leader, Sky Walker, and I have reached an informal understanding. He'll leave us alone as long as we leave his people alone."

"How many are living in the mountains?" Silk asked.

"Chata, a half Apache, half Mexican woman living at the rancho, says there are more than one hundred. I think the number fluctuates as families flee from the reservations and others go back," James pointed out. "Sky Walker told me he does not allow raiding parties to live with his band, and I believe him."

Victoria stared out her picture window and thought for a moment. "What if Sky Walker is killed or deposed? How will it affect our ranch?"

"We would know if a change takes place. Chata is used as a messenger by Sky Walker and by me, and she keeps me informed. I'll see that Rafael initiates the same relationship with her."

"It sounds as if our ranch is in a precarious position. But, if you think it will work, let's move ahead," Victoria emphasized.

"There is one other problem that I haven't mentioned yet. It also involves Don Ramon Aragon," James explained. He told Victoria and Silk about falling in love with Christina and learning that her fiancé preferred men to women.

"She told me that she was going through with the marriage because Miguel Soto's family and the Aragons were to partner in mining operations in northern Mexico. The union of the two families through marriage was very important to her father in Spain. She felt obligated and would accept the arranged marriage."

There was silence as Silk and Victoria starred at James, not knowing what to say.

"Now I think she has changed her mind. The last thing she said to me before I went to face the Apaches was, 'Come back for me when this is over.'"

"What are you going to do?" Silk asked.

His eyes narrowed as he looked at Silk and then at Victoria. "I'm going back for her!"

Victoria's mind was moving at top speed. "Then would you bring her back here to live?"

"Yes. It would be too dangerous for us to stay in Mexico. We would be married and raise a family here."

Those words brought a smile to Victoria's lips. "I'm in favor of that!"

CHAPTER 17

The following morning Silk and Cap Ousterhout were preparing to leave to determine how many of the Barringer cattle had been rustled and where they were taken. James approached the two men, and they talked briefly about tracking the cattle to a probable staging area from which the outlaws would move the cattle northward to the Tucson railhead.

"We should be able to determine how many there are and then plan some type of a surprise for them," Silk noted.

"That's what I would do," James stated.

"A number of the Barringer cowboys are Civil War veterans like me. They're good with guns," Silk pointed out.

"You are in charge. Do as you see fit," Barringer emphasized. "If you take any prisoners, hang them. No one rustles cattle from our ranch and lives."

James watched as the two men rode away. By mid-morning the supply column was ready to depart. Victoria was on her balcony watching the scene unfold below her as they prepared to leave. She motioned for James to join her. He walked up the stairs to the balcony and smiled at his grandmother.

"When I see you next, I hope to have Christina Aragon with me."

"I look forward to that, James. You remind me so much of Charles. If he were alive he would be very proud of his grandson, I know I am," she stated in a soft voice.

James smiled. He never asked for praise nor sought it, but hearing it from his grandmother was most welcome. He gave Victoria a hug, then went back downstairs and mounted Oro.

Barringer led the supply column until near nightfall when they stopped, campfires were built, and food prepared for the wagon drivers and guards. In all, twenty men were in the supply column, with eight cowboys acting as scouts and guards. The following morning, they prepared for the day long journey across the border to Rancho Vista Bonita, and by nightfall the hacienda came into view.

Rafael rode out to greet them, and the brothers got off their horses and embraced.

"Is that the way you dress in the Arizona Territory?" his brother asked. "You look like a cowboy with that Stetson and plain clothing."

"I've got my other clothes in the wagon. Remember, I'm running a crew of Arizona cowboys. I have to dress the part."

Rafael's English was good and he was able to get the wagons unloaded and supplies put in various buildings around the main house. Chata and some of the other women cooked for the Arizona cowboys. The following morning, the Barringer cowboys headed back to the Arizona ranch, leaving five of the wagons to be used at the rancho.

"Now, that's the brother I recognize," said a smiling Rafael after James changed into his Mexican clothing. "I have some plans I want you to look at for expansion of the main house."

"Good. You've always had an artist's skills for drawing. I

want to send Chata to meet with Sky Walker. Let's talk with her first."

Chata was in the kitchen when the brothers entered. "I would like you to take a message to Sky Walker. I brought some supplies including hoes, shovels, and other tools that I would like to give him. I will take them up to the mountain, along with some cattle. Ask him if he will meet with Rafael and me."

Chata nodded her head in agreement. Her stoic demeanor did not change, and she showed no emotion. "I will leave now."

"Do you want to ride a horse?" asked Rafael.

"I don't ride horses," she said, and moved swiftly out of the room.

"She's your connection to Sky Walker and the Apaches. Chata keeps close watch on everything," said Ricardo.

Rafael appeared skeptical. "You've told me before that an agreement will work, but I find it hard to believe. The only Apaches I've ever had contact with were at the end of my gun."

Ricardo smiled. "You will be surprised at the man's character. He is highly intelligent, complex, and an in-depth thinker."

"What is he doing here in the mountains? Why doesn't he govern his people while living on the reservation?"

"Rafael, they want freedom. It's that simple. If you don't have freedom, you don't have anything."

The brothers spread a large drawing on a table and talked about Rafael's ideas for renovation and additions to the hacienda. The existing building was typical of the times, an L-shaped structure with three long rooms on a north-south line and a fourth room extending west. Right at the juncture of the L was an inside well. The roof was flat with a surrounding parapet three feet high. The walls were massive — twenty-four inches thick — and helped to conserve heat during the winters and keep the house cool in the hot months. Inside, the rooms were twenty feet wide with beamed ceilings, and had covered patios extending to the open courtyard. The height of the building was sixteen feet.

Rafael's renovation ideas were extensive. He proposed extending the short arm of the L and then adding another long line of rooms the entire length of the home on the other side of the central courtyard. The fourth side would be a tall wall and parapet.

Enclosed within the structure would be a well. Just outside the end of the rancho would be a stable, carriage house, and tack room. The parapet wall and walkway would extend around the entire rectangular structure for quick movement by defenders in time of attack. A corral, large enough to hold several hundred cattle or horses, would be erected to the east of the home.

A large barracks to house the vaqueros would be constructed near the main house. Other nearby structures would include a smoke house where hams and sides of bacon would be cured, vats for rendering lard, a wagon and harness repair shop, and a commissary building from which employees would draw supplies.

"You didn't miss a thing," Ricardo mused.

"Well, you and I built a lot of structures at Salazar's rancho. We both know what will work and what won't."

"It looks good to me. Get started as soon as you can. I'll see that additional supplies and lumber are sent to you from the Barringer Ranch as you ask for them."

"Ask your grandmother if we could borrow a couple of

carpenters to guide us in putting down wood floors."

The brothers inspected the existing house and found it solid. The surrounding adobe homes were quickly being renovated, and others built by the dozens of peons who had come from Don Ramon's rancho. Several kilns were turning out adobe blocks.

At the end of the day, Chata returned and approached the brothers. "He said he will meet you tomorrow at noon where the two of you spoke before."

"Did you tell him my brother, Rafael, would be coming with me?"

"Yes. He is expecting both of you," she said in an even, monotone voice.

Chata turned and walked to the kitchen.

"I get the idea that she hates Mexicans," Rafael noted.

"I don't know her history, but you may be correct."

Rafael laughed. "That fat husband of hers does nothing but sleep. I haven't seen him with his eyes open yet. He sleeps all day, all afternoon, and I assume, all evening. She takes meals to him, and he eats like he's starving and then falls back asleep."

"It's a wonder the huge chair he's sitting in doesn't break down," Ricardo said, and laughed.

"When he dies, we'll have the peons pick up the chair with him in it and bury the two of them together," Rafael joked.

After dinner, the brothers sat on the porch drinking beer.

"So, you are really in love this time?" Rafael asked.

Ricardo shook his head in agreement. "Yes. It hurts me to think about her. The wedding to Miguel Soto is scheduled to take place in about three weeks."

"Do you feel more strongly about her than Don Carlos Bustamante's daughter, Maria?"

"I really cared for Maria, but my feelings for Christina are much stronger."

"Do you have any idea what you are going to do?"

Ricardo exhaled sharply. "No. But, I know she wants me to come for her."

"Be careful, brother. My guess is that she will be under heavy guard."

CHAPTER 18

Late the following morning, Rafael and Ricardo started the trek towards the mountains behind the hacienda. A vaquero drove the wagon filled with tools and supplies. Three other Mexican cowboys brought a small herd of cattle along at a leisurely pace.

When they could go no higher with the wagon, it was unloaded. The cattle were left feeding in a small meadow, and the vaqueros returned to the rancho as the brothers began the slow ascent along a narrow trail.

"I can feel eyes on me," Rafael said.

"Yes. I know what you mean."

Once they reached the open area where the first meeting had taken place, the brothers dismounted and put their gun belts over the saddle horns. Moments later, Sky Walker emerged from behind a rock outcropping.

Rafael stared at the Indian chief. His black hair fell almost to his shoulders and was held in place by a wide band around his forehead. Sky Walker's large face was covered with wrinkles and crevices brought on by years in the sun. His eyes were slits with pouches underneath, and a big, strong nose was the focal point on his face. Sky Walker's lips curled down at the corners, and his granite-like chin finished off the appearance of a face chiseled in marble.

"Thank you for meeting with us," said Ricardo.

"How can I help you?" Sky Walker stated.

"I wanted you to meet my brother, Rafael, who is one of the owners of Vista Bonita. He will be here on a regular basis, and is the man in charge."

"I see."

"We will be doing much construction at the rancho, building a larger main house and more surrounding buildings. Vaqueros and cowboys from the Arizona Territory will come and go with supplies and building materials, but no one will come into the mountains to bother you."

"It is as we agreed," said Sky Walker. "Are those tools and cattle for us that you brought with you?"

"Yes, out of respect."

Sky Walker turned and motioned to the yet unseen Apaches in the rocks to claim the prizes.

"There will be a detachment of Mexican soldiers arriving at the rancho within days, I think. It has nothing to do with your people. All of these families of peons came from the rancho of Don Ramon Aragon. They no longer want to live there. Don Ramon may try to take them back, and the army may back him."

"I know about the attacks on the two ranchos by the raiding parties," said Sky Walker.

"Then you know that your son was killed," Ricardo noted.

This statement hit Rafael like a club. *Mother of God, Ricardo! You didn't tell me*, he thought. But wisely, his expression did not change.

"I know."

"We buried the Apaches killed in the dynamite blast at the rancho. I recognized your son and had his body wrapped in canvas and buried at a curve in the Big Sandy Creek, two miles east of the rancho."

Ricardo kneeled down and drew a picture of the creek where it made an S-curve.

"This is the spot where he is buried. There is a black cross at the location. I assume you will want to retrieve his body for a ceremonial burial."

"Yes."

Ricardo stood up and the two men looked into each others' eyes.

"Thank you," said Sky Walker.

"I hope you can use the supplies and the cattle. Let Chata know if anything else is needed."

"We have fought each other for years. You have proven to be an honorable man," said the chief.

"And you have proven to be an honorable man, Sky Walker."

Sky Walker turned to Rafael. "If your word is as good as your brother's, I will keep my end of the agreement."

"It has been my pleasure to meet you," said Rafael.

The Apache chief turned and walked behind the rock out cropping and disappeared.

The Montoya brothers strapped on their holsters and mounted their horses. "Don't say anything until we get out of the mountains. The rock walls have ears," Ricardo warned.

Once they were back on the slopes of the mountain, Rafael could contain himself no longer.

"You killed his son, and you didn't tell me!" he exclaimed. "I thought I would piss in my pants when you said that!"

"If I had told you, you might have been very

uncomfortable."

"Mother of God! Uncomfortable! I could just feel an arrow in my back."

"He was killed in the dynamite blast," Ricardo explained.

Rafael took a deep breath and whistled. "I'm glad that's over. You understand these Apaches better than I do."

***

At mid-morning the following day, the brothers were alerted to dust coming from an approaching column of horsemen. They climbed to the top of the ranch building and stood behind the parapet wall, watching the oncoming soldiers and vaqueros.

"How many are there?"

Ricardo studied the horsemen. "About thirty-five, I think. The tables are set up. I'll try to get Don Ramon and the officers to sit with us while we discuss what transpired," said Ricardo. "Don't respond to Don Ramon's insults or accusations. He is an angry, arrogant bastard, so we must respond with dignity, logic, and facts. If the army officers think we are honorable men, we may be able to persuade them that our explanations are true."

"I understand. If we get into a shouting match, nothing will be accomplished," Rafael stated.

***

Don Ramon's coach pulled up in front of the hacienda. The door opened and the angry little man jumped out. He was followed out of the coach by two army officers, a lieutenant and a major.

"You destroyed my rancho! You destroyed my mine! You stole my workers! You rotten bastard!" he shouted at Ricardo.

"It's nice to see you, Don Ramon," Montoya said in a calm voice.

"I want him arrested for destroying my property! Put him in irons!" he yelled at the army officers.

"Perhaps we could all sit down here and discuss the details of what happened," Ricardo stated in a smooth manner. "This is my brother, Rafael."

Lieutenant Fernando Solano looked at his superior officer, Major Miguel Alhambra, who was undecided as to what course of action to take.

"Major, why don't we sit down and talk through what occurred?" Solano recommended.

"That's my recommendation," said Major Alhambra in an authoritarian voice.

The five men took seats. Don Ramon sat at the head of the table facing Alhambra, who sat at the other end. Rafael and Ricardo sat side by side, with Rafael as a buffer between Ricardo and Don Ramon. Solano sat opposite the brothers.

"Make no mistake, I'm taking all of these people back with me. They need to get busy rebuilding my rancho," said the angry don.

Ricardo looked first at Major Alhambra and then at Lieutenant Solano. "I would like to tell you what occurred at the rancho, from the time I arrived there to warn Don Ramon about the impending attack by nearly seventy Apaches, to the end of the raid," Ricardo stated. "On the evening I warned Don Ramon about the coming raid, he decided to leave in his carriage with his guests, accompanied by all of his bodyguards and vaqueros. He was going to leave the peons to die rather than stay and fight."

Don Ramon jumped to his feet. "Lies! All lies! You can't believe anything this bastard says."

"His niece forced him to leave about a dozen vaqueros with me before they departed. She told him she would not marry a business associate of Don Ramon's unless he allowed the vaqueros to make up their own minds about staying or leaving. We could have used the other fifteen fighting men, but they left with the don."

"My private business is not to be discussed here!" the don shouted.

"Don Ramon, would you explain what occurred if it differs from what Don Ricardo has stated?" Solano said.

"I won't be questioned by a mere lieutenant. Besides, this man is not a don. He's a gringo."

The two officers looked at Ricardo with surprise.

"It's true that I was born in the Arizona Territory to Anglo parents who died during a stagecoach attack. My mother hid me in the rocks before they murdered her. My Mexican father saw what happened from his nearby camp and took me to Mexico, where he raised me as his own son. I didn't find out about my true heritage until my father, Gustavo, was dying. Rafael and I always thought we were blood brothers."

"That's a ridiculous story. You are not a Mexican, and you can not own this rancho," Don Ramon stuttered.

"I have dual citizenship. And Rafael has authentic citizenship," Ricardo explained. He reached into his vest pocket and produced the legalized and properly signed and documented papers. He passed them to the major.

Major Alhambra took a few moments to read through the documents. "These appear to be in order," the major stated in a strong voice.

"Perhaps we should return to the raid on Don Ramon's rancho," Lieutenant Solano recommended.

"Yes. We should get back to that," said Major Alhambra.

"After Don Ramon left with most of his men, I felt that the only way to protect the peons was to gather them at the mine, where we could direct gunfire out of the mine at the Apaches. It took us most of the night to transport the men, women, and children to the mine, and we arrived before daybreak. By that time, the Apaches had been alerted and attacked us, and we were able to drive them away from the entrance, killing a number of the Indians. A number of the ranchers were also killed."

The army officers seemed fascinated by the story, studying Ricardo as he spoke.

"This is all garbage! Why are we listening to this fiction?" Don Ramon complained.

"There was an air shaft leading out of the mine. Three vaqueros and I climbed out and watched as the Apaches brought large quantities of dynamite up to the mine. We fired at the dynamite, and the explosion killed about three-quarters of the braves," Montoya recounted.

"Have you ever heard a more ridiculous story? This man will say anything to cover the fact that he blew up my rancho!" Don Ramon snorted.

"There were blood spots all around the mine entrance. How do you explain that, Don Ramon?" Solano asked, acting as a buffer for his commanding officer by asking embarrassing questions.

Aragon's eyes widened and his face turned bright red. "You are nothing but a lieutenant, and you should not be questioning my word! I am Don Ramon Aragon, and my friends are the politicians who control the army in Hermosillo. And don't you ever forget it!"

"No one is questioning your word, Don Ramon. And we know that you have friends in high places," said Lieutenant Solano in a firm voice.

"Let's get back to Don Ricardo's story," said Major

Alhambra.

Ricardo continued. "After that explosion, the remaining Apaches loaded up all kinds of supplies on pack horses and left. Of the more than seventy Apaches involved in the raid, only ten or twelve remained alive and escaped."

"Do you have any idea where they went?" the lieutenant asked.

"Probably back to the reservations in the Arizona Territory. They like to share with their families," said Ricardo.

"Well, you've listened to this ridiculous story, and now it's time to arrest this man for blowing up my hacienda and mine and stealing my peons," said Don Ramon.

"One thing is not clear. Who did blow up the mine and Don Ramon's headquarters building?" Solano asked.

For the first time, Ricardo leaned back in his chair and laughed. "The mine and the rancho exploded after we had buried the Apaches and were on the trail to my hacienda. Several miners and vaqueros went back and finished the job as retribution for being left to die. I told the families that they could stay and wait for Don Ramon to return, or come and live on our rancho. No one wanted to stay."

Don Ramon's face turned a brighter color of red. "You bastard! You are so full of lies. We all know the truth," he yelled. "I want my peons and miners back, and I want them back there now!"

"They are free to live wherever they want, according to our constitution," Solano pointed out.

"I'm going to tell you for the last time, lieutenant, assemble those peons and bring them back to my ranch. And arrest that man!" he shouted, pointing at Ricardo.

Lieutenant Solano turned to his superior officer. "Perhaps we should talk for a few moments." The two army officers got up from the table and moved towards the front patio stairs.

"You aren't going to leave me here with these Montoya brothers, are you?" Aragon asked in a worried voice, eyes darting from Ricardo to Rafael.

"Well, you can go and sit in your carriage if you would like," said Solano. Don Ramon jumped up from his chair and ran to the carriage and the safety of his bodyguards.

The army officers conferred in low voices. "I think the peons will verify Don Ricardo's story. If we arrest him on bogus charges, the truth would come out in court. This would make the two of us look bad in the eyes of our army superiors," the quick-minded lieutenant pointed out.

"I can't see where there are charges to be brought against Don Ricardo. But, our orders are to return the peons to his rancho. They are written orders that must be followed," Major Alhambra emphasized.

"Major, can you imagine the punishment that will be administered to those peons? I think he will kill some of them as a warning to the others not to leave again."

"We are bound by our orders. That's that," said Alhambra.

"If you would like, I will question some of the peons about the particulars of Don Ricardo's story just to enhance our written report," Solano said.

"Yes, question the peons."

***

During the next hour, Lieutenant Solano questioned numerous peons. All of them substantiated the facts and said they would be dead if it weren't for Ricardo's quick actions. Don Ramon continued to get in and out of his carriage several times. He would look to see who Solano was questioning, then climb into the carriage, then out. Aragon asked for water, went to the bathroom, and climbed back into the carriage.

"Nervous, isn't he?" said a grinning Rafael. "What is your guess about how the army officers will rule?"

"It depends on what their orders are."

***

The two army officers conferred again after Solano finished questioning the peons. Then they walked to the patio and sat down in their chairs. Don Ramon came running from his carriage and took his seat, breathing hard from the exertion.

"Don Ramon, the peons have substantiated Don Ricardo's story. What do you have to say that would contradict the facts as they were presented to us?" Lieutenant Solano asked.

"Everything is a lie. He went to my rancho, blew everything up, and stole my peons and miners! It's my word against his!" he cried out.

"That's not what the facts would indicate," Lieutenant Solano pointed out. "In fact, you may owe him a debt of gratitude for saving the lives of the men, women, and children on your rancho."

"Preposterous! You are a low life lieutenant! You can't talk to me like that! When I get back to Hermosillo, I'll see that you are busted in rank," Aragon shouted.

"If you have no further information for us regarding the Apache attack, our decision is that no charges will be brought against Don Ricardo," the lieutenant concluded.

"That decision is final," Major Alhambra stated loudly.

"What about my peons?" Aragon asked in a frantic voice. "I need them to rebuild. Otherwise, I will have to buy more from other dons."

"Our written orders are to accompany the peons back to Don Ramon's rancho. This we will do," said Major Alhambra. "We have no choice."

Don Ramon jumped to his feet. "They are going back!

175

And I will teach them a lesson they will never forget!"

The two army officers started to rise from their chairs.

"Ten thousand American dollars!" Ricardo stated loudly.

Don Ramon froze in his tracks, his eyes open wide. "What do you mean?" he blurted.

"I mean I will pay you ten thousand American dollars for services rendered. The price is not negotiable. The funds will be sent from the Barringer Ranch tomorrow to the Hermosillo Bank. The money will be deposited in your account there. It should take a couple of days to arrive. In return, you will renounce all rights to the peons who left your rancho," Montoya replied.

Don Ramon's mind was churning, eyes blinking, sweat rolling down his face. He reasoned that he could buy five hundred peons for that amount of money, or buy one hundred and fifty farmers and miners and pocket the remainder of the money. Or, he could bill Miguel Soto's family for the entire cost and keep the whole ten thousand dollars for himself. *Yes, I like that idea the best*, he thought. His eyes narrowed. "What guarantee do I have that you will keep your end of the bargain?" Aragon snarled.

"I have three identical agreements drawn up here to be signed by all five of us sitting around this table," Ricardo explained. He handed one document to Don Ramon and a second to the army officers. Rafael was staring at his brother as if he thought he had lost his mind.

The agreement stated, "To Whom It May Concern: I, Ricardo Montoya, agree to pay Don Ramon Aragon the sum of ten thousand American dollars to be deposited in his Hermosillo bank account within four days. This is for services rendered. In return, Don Ramon Aragon agrees to permanently drop any and all efforts to reclaim the men, women, and children who left his rancho and are now living on the rancho owned by Rafael and Ricardo Montoya."

"What do you mean, 'services rendered'?" Aragon asked in a suspicious voice.

"That's for giving us your recommendations for fighting Apaches," Ricardo said with a straight face.

Aragon squinted his eyes as he tried to determine if Ricardo was serious. Rafael turned his head, bent over, and began coughing loudly in order to keep from laughing. The army officers looked at each other and found it difficult to keep from smiling.

"Where do I sign?" Aragon said loudly, greed and arrogance conquering dignity.

Three copies were passed around the table and signed by all five men. Alhambra kept one, Don Ramon the second, and Rafael received the third.

"What guarantee do I have that you will keep your word?" a suddenly suspicious Don Ramon blurted out a second time.

"If I don't, these army officers can come back here, arrest me, and take the peons back to your ranch," said Ricardo.

"That's true," said Major Alhambra.

Don Ramon beamed. "Let's get out of here, gentlemen. I have been vindicated! And I have been paid for the treachery and deceit heaped upon me by this stinking gringo!"

The men rose from their chairs and Aragon ran over to his carriage, looking back suspiciously as if he might be chased, and climbed inside. He looked out the window and yelled. "I don't want that lieutenant in my carriage. Let him ride a horse!"

The Montoya brothers shook hands with the army officers and exchanged farewells. "It was a pleasure meeting you," said Lieutenant Solano. "Major Alhambra and I would like to say more, but protocol dictates otherwise." He smiled, walked over to his soldiers who were lounging in the shade, and ordered them to saddle their mounts for the return trip. A half hour later the column of men departed.

***

"When did you draw up those papers?" Rafael asked.

"Last night after you went to bed. If I had told you what I might do, we would have had a long, drawn out argument. And I just didn't want that."

"You're right, we would have. That's a lot of money. We could have negotiated the figure down," Rafael reasoned.

"You're probably correct, but what price do you put on a man's life? If we had not put this agreement together, he would have killed several of the peons when he arrived back at his rancho just to prove a point. I didn't want to take the chance," Ricardo noted.

Rafael was still not convinced. "That was too much money."

"The first large cattle drive that we take up to the railroad in Tucson will net us more than double that amount. And you now have a large number of workers to begin the restoration," Ricardo pointed out.

Rafael grinned. "Yes. And, there are a couple of lovely young ladies in the group who have been smiling at me. I'll have to make their acquaintance."

The brothers spent the rest of the afternoon going over plans for reconstruction of the rancho, and Rafael put together a list of materials and tools to be sent to him. The following day a rider from the north arrived at the ranch house at full gallop. The cowboy jumped off his horse, ran into the hacienda, and handed a note to Ricardo.

It read, *Cap Ousterhout is dead. Silk has been wounded. We need you. Victoria.*

CHAPTER 19

"What the hell happened?" Rafael asked after he read the note.

"I sent them in blind to investigate the rustling of some of our cattle. They didn't know what to expect." Ricardo began pacing, his mind working at top speed, then turned to the cowboy. "Ride back as quickly as you can and tell my grandmother that I have to make one stop first to gather information about the rustlers. Then I'll come back to the ranch. Tell her not to send anyone to investigate until I get back."

The cowhand was given two fresh horses, food, and water, and sent on his way.

"Where are we headed?" asked Rafael.

"Not we. You need to stay here and oversee these dozens and dozens of men and women. There's no telling what would happen to them if you aren't here."

Rafael grimaced. He saw the logic in Ricardo's reasoning. "You're right. Where are you going?"

"I told you about those Baca brothers who had beaten Paco Flores. I busted them up pretty good. Paco suspected they were riding with a gang of rustlers using a small ranch north of Sasabe as headquarters. That would have been in the same general area that Cap and Silk rode to. I'm going to get information out of them one way or another."

Ricardo made the trip to The Crossing in record time, alternating between two horses and arriving shortly before ten at night, and went directly to the cantina where Paco was recuperating. Ricardo walked in, drawing gazes from the vaqueros drinking and playing cards, including the Baca brothers sitting at one of the tables, and approached the bartender.

"Is Paco Flores in back?

The thin Mexican scowled. "Yeah."

Ricardo decided not to go in back, thinking the brothers might leave before he returned. "Go get Paco," Montoya ordered.

"I don't take orders from you, and I can't leave the bar," he growled.

"The bar is closing," Montoya stated emphatically.

"What the hell...?" Before he could finish his sentence, Ricardo grabbed him by the front of his shirt and pulled him halfway over the bar. "Go get Paco Flores, now!" The customers were quiet, not speaking, just staring at the tall vaquero. Ricardo pushed the bartender backward and he hurried away to get Flores. Ricardo looked around slowly from one table to the next. The men averted their eyes as Montoya looked at them. Seeing no threat, Montoya announced, "The bar is closed! Everybody out!" The men got up from their chairs, some slowly, some quite fast, and headed for the door.

"Not you two," he said to the Baca brothers.

The brothers were beginning to stand and froze in their positions. One brother had his head covered in bandages, the other had his arm wrapped. Both had their ribs encased in bandages from the beatings they had sustained.

Paco Flores walked slowly into the bar, followed by the bartender. Ricardo looked directly into the bartender's eyes, and the man saw the anger that was smoldering within Montoya.

"Leave us," Ricardo ordered.

The bartender quickly turned around and went into the back room

Paco took one look at Montoya and recognized that he was furious. "What has happened, my friend?" he asked.

"I'm going to question the Baca brothers about the outlaw gang they're involved with," he said, and turned to the brothers. Jose Baca had an angry look on his face, but his brother, Pepe, appeared frightened. Montoya walked over to the table where they were sitting. "I have some questions for you. If you answer them, no harm will come to you."

"What do you want to know?" asked a worried Pepe.

"Shut up!" his brother told him. "Don't say nothing!"

In one swift movement, Ricardo drew his revolver and smashed Jose across the forehead. The young man went over backwards in his chair and landed on the floor in a semi-conscious state. Montoya knew which one he wanted to question.

"My God, Ricardo! What are you doing?" Flores said loudly.

"Relax, Paco. I'm not going to hurt this kid," Montoya said in a loud voice. He turned his attention to the terrified Pepe, whose eyes were wide and his mouth open.

"You have ridden with an outlaw band that works from a small ranch near Sasabe. Several hundred cattle from the Barringer Ranch were rustled and driven in that direction. I own the ranch and sent my best tracker and my foreman to investigate. One was killed and the other was wounded. Do you understand so far?"

The young man shook his head yes, but was too frightened to respond.

"My first question is, who is the outlaw leader?"

"He'll kill me if I say anything!" Baca blurted out.

Ricardo grabbed him by his shirt collar.

"Boy, look at me! I'll kill you if you don't!"

Staring into Montoya's angry eyes, Pepe made an instantaneous decision. "His name is Vic Norris."

"How many men, excluding you and your brother, are riding with him?"

"About fifteen," he replied in a voice that cracked.

"Is he driving the stolen cattle to Tucson and the railhead?"

Pepe's eyes were wide and sweat poured down his face. "Yes. Vic waits until he has about fifteen hundred head and then makes the drive, but doesn't use normal trails."

"How soon will the next drive be made?"

"I don't know."

"Guess."

"Maybe a week."

Montoya turned to Flores, who was listening intently. "My tracker, Cap, was the best man I have ever seen in that business. My foreman, Silk Mathews, is fast and accurate with a revolver and rifle. Up close, they could handle any men," Ricardo noted. "Cap is dead, Silk is wounded." His attention returned to Baca. "Does he have any top gunmen in the group?"

"There's a couple who are fast draws. There's also a long range shooter who has one of those rifles with a scope."

"Go on."

Pepe suddenly seemed to realize he was volunteering too much information, his face reflecting mental anguish and fear. Ricardo reached forward and grabbed him by the shoulder, causing the youth to cry out in pain and terror. "Answer my questions and I won't hurt you!" he declared, eyes blazing and mouth tightly shut in a firm line.

"Norris has him backtracking and shooting at anyone following the trail of rustled cattle. He's really good," Pepe said hurriedly, using his sleeve to wipe his sweaty face.

"So, his job is to persuade the pursuers not to follow?"

"Yeah, I guess so."

"That might explain what happened," Montoya said to Flores. "What is the shooter's name?"

"You won't tell anyone I told you?" Pepe asked in a worried voice.

"No one will know," Ricardo assured him.

"Villalobos."

Montoya looked momentarily confused. "I killed a man named Villalobos months ago," he emphasized.

"I know he had a brother who was killed," Baca said.

"What is this shooter's first name?"

"Fausto. He keeps a rifle with a scope in a long, leather case. He either has it slung over his shoulder or hung from the saddle horn when he rides," said Pepe.

"How many Anglos and how many Mexicans are in the band?" Ricardo asked.

Pepe thought for a moment. "Jose and me and Villalobos and two others are Mexican. There's about ten Anglos."

"What does this Vic Norris look like?"

"He has a black beard, big nose, and black hair that he keeps in a ponytail. Norris rode with Quantrill's Raiders. He's a mean one."

Montoya turned to Flores. "Are there other questions you can think of?"

Paco shook his head no.

Ricardo grabbed Pepe by the front of his shirt and pulled him upright. Pepe's eyes widened in fear. "Don't hurt me!"

"Find yourself another line of work! I'm going to shoot or hang every one of those rustlers! Since you and your brother were not with the gang when my ranch hands were shot, I'll let you live."

Their faces were close together. Pepe looked into the smoldering eyes of the tall man and found it hard to breathe.

Paco walked up to the two men. "Pepe, make sure you convince your brother. You won't live long in the rustling business."

Jose finally regained consciousness and raised himself up on one elbow. "Don't tell him anything, Pepe," he said in a garbled voice.

Ricardo and Paco walked back to his room.

"How have they been treating you?"

"Like royalty. They clean my room everyday, and the food is the absolute best," Flores said, and smiled.

"Is Marcos Baca taking care of the stables?"

"Yes. It's operating very smoothly."

"I'll change clothes and go. Can you have a messenger take a letter to my grandmother, Victoria Barringer?"

"Sure," Paco replied.

Montoya wrote a letter telling her to transfer ten thousand dollars to Ramon Aragon's account in the Hermosillo Bank as quickly as possible. He said he would be back at the Barringer Ranch in a day or two. Ricardo borrowed a pair of binoculars from Flores and changed into Arizona cowboy clothing.

"Go with God, Ricardo," Paco stated.

"God will not ride with me on this day," said Montoya, who had now become James Barringer.

By midday he had traveled to the Sasabe area, skirted the community, and continued north to the turn off where he had been told the small ranch was located. James circled around to the rear of the ranch house and bunkhouse and began surveillance. He watched men saddle and unsaddle their horses in a large corral as they came and went from the ranch. James did not see anyone who looked like Vic Norris, nor was there a rider carrying a gun case. It was near dusk when Norris rode into the ranch accompanied by Villalobos. The shooter took the leather case off the saddle and the two men entered the ranch house. *Villalobos has the same dark, oval face as his brother, Alfredo*, James thought. *They're two of a kind.*

That night, Barringer ate a cold dinner and bedded down. The following morning James was awake before sunrise, saddled his horse, and waited. Shortly after the sun came up, Villalobos walked outside carrying his gun case, saddled his horse, and rode off. James stayed well to the rear of the shooter and out of sight. Twice Villalobos stopped his horse and used his binoculars to review the terrain in front. Once he dismounted on top of a rise and scoped the area behind. *He's a careful one*, James thought to himself.

An hour later Villalobos seemed to find the vantage point he was looking for, made himself comfortable in the rocks, and waited. James assumed he wanted to see if any other riders would be coming from the direction of the Barringer Ranch. By late afternoon he was apparently satisfied that no riders would be coming that day, so he mounted and used his binoculars to survey the return route, not spotting Barringer, who was well hidden in the boulder-strewn rocky terrain. Villalobos began the return trip, and had started to pass

James's location when he again stopped and reviewed the return route with binoculars. The killer took his rifle out of the leather case and continued forward at a slow pace, something causing him to be suspicious.

When the assassin was about seventy-five feet away, James stood up and took careful aim just as Villalobos spotted him. Barringer fired a split second before the shooter got off a snap shot that sailed past James's right ear. Barringer's bullet smashed into Villalobos's right shoulder, the impact causing the shooter to drop his rifle. Villalobos reached around with his left hand to pull his revolver from the holster on his right side, but James's next bullet hit the gunman in the left shoulder and knocked him off his horse. He crawled around on the ground, trying to pick up his revolver with a hand that was not working. The assassin was on his knees, snarling and swearing with his useless arms hanging down. His dark eyes mirrored loathing and hatred as Barringer advanced slowly with his rifle under his arm.

"Who are you?" he called out in a harsh, grating voice, coughing, mouth hanging open.

"My name is James Barringer. I was the one who killed your brother. Those two men you shot worked for me on the Barringer Ranch."

"I felt someone was back there," he growled.

James bound up Villalobos's wounds to stop the bleeding. Villalobos's face was distorted with pain. "What the hell are you doing? Finish it!" the shooter snarled.

"Not just yet." Barringer put a rope around his neck and encircled a rock outcropping above him. He pulled Villalobos to his feet and tightened the rope, causing the outlaw to gurgle.

"How soon is Norris moving the herd north?"

"Screw you!"

Barringer tightened the rope until the shooter was standing on the tips of his toes, yelling from the pain. "Tell me what I want to know, and it'll be over fast."

"I'll see you in hell, you son of a bitch!" the killer snarled. James tried the rope trick a few more times, but the outlaw would not reveal any information.

"Did you watch the sunrise this morning?" Barringer asked him.

"What the hell are you talking about?" said Villalobos in a scratchy voice.

"Every man should before he dies," James said with a note of finality in his voice.

Then the rancher pulled the rope tight, which lifted the outlaw off his feet. The shooter's feet kicked wildly as James secured the rope and let the assassin die slowly. He put Villalobos's rifle back in the gun case and walked both horses up to the dead man. James tied the lifeless body over Villalobos's saddle and began the trip to the Barringer Ranch.

CHAPTER 20

James dismounted in front of the Barringer headquarters. Victoria and Silk emerged from the home, Silk using a crutch, his left leg heavily bandaged.

"This is the shooter named Villalobos who killed Cap and shot you," James told Silk.

"The shot struck Cap in the chest, and he was dead before he hit the ground," Silk explained. "I dismounted, ran over to him, took a slug in the leg, and hid in the rocks until nightfall before bringing Cap back here. I didn't hear the shot until after the bullet hit me."

James had Villalobos's body taken to the stables. They walked to the large downstairs office and sat around the conference table while James explained about stopping at The Crossing and prying information out of Pepe Baca.

"I stayed concealed and waited until the next morning when Villalobos appeared, carrying a rifle case. I figured if you were hit, it probably was from long range," James explained.

"Yeah, it was," the blond haired foreman replied.

"Villalobos backtracked to determine if anyone else was coming from our ranch, and spent the day waiting for whoever might appear. I nailed him on his return trip, shot him twice, but couldn't make him talk. I finally hung him and then brought his body back here. We'll let the outlaws speculate about what happened to him."

"What's your plan?" Victoria asked, reasoning that her grandson would take swift action.

"I think the rustlers are about ready to move the herd north to Tucson and the railhead. We'll intercept them before they reach Tucson," James indicated.

"Why wouldn't they go to one of the nearby army forts?' Victoria asked.

"The army won't buy cattle that have altered brands or brands they recognize. They sure wouldn't buy any cattle from this crew. The cattle buyers at the railhead don't care; they just count out the money, load the cattle, and the train departs," Barringer explained.

"How many are in the outlaw band?" Silk asked.

"Fifteen or more."

The Barringer Ranch decision makers discussed James's idea about intercepting the rustlers. Just before the meeting adjourned, Victoria spoke up.

"I sent the ten thousand dollar bank draft to the Hermosillo Bank in Don Ramon Aragon's name, and the supplies Rafael asked for are on their way," Victoria noted. "He must be building a mansion with the amount of supplies he's requested."

"It'll be a big rancho, specifically designed to withstand Apache attacks," James maintained.

They briefly talked about Apache Chief Sky Walker and Don Ramon's appearance at the rancho with the military. "Giving him money was the only way to allow him to save face. Otherwise, the army officers' orders were to return the peons to Don Ramon's rancho," James explained.

"Will he make another attempt to retrieve them?" she asked.

James showed them the document that Don Ramon had signed.

"What does 'services rendered' mean?" Silk asked.

"That's what Don Ramon wanted to know. I told him it was for giving us his expertise on fighting Apaches."

Silk and Victoria both laughed. Then the conversation returned to the outlaws.

The following morning the pack horses were loaded, and the men prepared to depart. The entire crew was made up of cowboys, most of whom had served in the Civil War and knew how to handle side arms and rifles. Barringer gave the shooter's rifle with the scope to Silk, who sighted through the scope and was impressed. "I'll bet he was a sniper in the Civil War. I could knock someone off a horse a half mile away with this rifle," Silk noted. "He must have been surprised as hell when you shot him."

"I ambushed him at close range, and even then, he got a shot off. He was deadly," James noted. "I put a rope around his neck and kept hauling him up off the ground, but he wouldn't give me any information. So, I finally pulled him up and let him kick until he died. That was a pay back for you and Cap."

Silk nodded his head, understanding.

"I'm going to hang every one left alive after we ambush them," James declared.

Mathews studied his boss for several moments, realizing suppressed anger and hostility were just below the surface. *He's had a bad month*, Silk reasoned.

Barringer was reading Silk's mind. "Cap was a good man. These outlaws don't deserve any leniency. If you rustle cattle, you hang!" he emphasized.

"I'm not disagreeing with you. But a lot of killing changes a man. As I've told you, I was a captain in Jeb Stuart's cavalry. Sometimes I would lead two hundred or more men on raids and flanking movements for the army. We killed an awful lot of blue coats. Towards the end of the war, I began to question why Americans were killing Americans…it seemed so senseless. When the war ended, I wanted to get as far away as possible, and ended up here."

"What's your point?"

"The point is that I hated the sight of a blue uniform. I needed a change of scenery in order to start thinking normally again. This ranch work has straightened out my thoughts, and I think I'm fairly normal again," Silk contended.

James was silent as he thought about Silk's comments, then exhaled sharply. "It's a point well made."

***

Silk walked over to the men who were waiting by their mounts. Victoria motioned for James to join her on the veranda.

"Are you going straight down to Mexico when this confrontation is finished?" she asked.

"The wedding is scheduled to take place in about ten days. I don't want to get there the day after," James pointed out.

Victoria's eyes sparkled as she smiled.

"You will bring Christina here, I assume?"

"I'll try to. There's no guarantee that she'll break off her proposed marriage. But I'll sure try hard to convince her. And yes, we'll come back here," he said as he kissed her cheek.

***

The column with the pack horses and cowboys headed due west to where the outlaw band was thought to be using a small ranch north of Sasabe. They took a round about route that ended near a creek winding through a small valley three miles from the ranch house.

Silk had recommended an older cowboy named Dave Forrester as being a good second in command during the coming conflict. Forrester had white hair, a matching white moustache, and light blue eyes that gave him the look of a gentleman rather than a rugged cowboy. He and Cap Ousterhout had been good friends, and he was anxious to avenge the tracker's death. Barringer and Forrester left the group of cowboys after they made camp, and worked their way up behind the ranch house as the sun was setting.

"I was thinking there would be guards since Villalobos didn't return," James said.

"There's no lantern lit in the bunk house," Dave pointed out. "There's no one in there."

They could see smoke coming from the small ranch house chimney, and the building was lighted.

"Do you think it's a trap?" Forrester asked.

"I don't think so. It doesn't feel like people are here."

The two men glanced at each other and Forrester shrugged his shoulders. He'd been a Confederate combat sergeant during the Civil War and participated in numerous scouting forays and battles.

"There's one way to find out. I'll work my way up to the door, and we'll see if anyone is home. Keep me covered," James said in a quiet voice.

At that moment, the door opened and a grizzled old man shuffled out. He threw a pan of water into the bushes, rolled a cigarette, and smoked it slowly. James realized he had only one leg, the other being a wooden prosthesis that was a poorly fitted replacement for his missing limb. His hair was scraggly, salt and pepper in color, as was his beard. He looked tired, as if he needed to sit down and rest. When he hobbled back inside, James worked his way down from the hillside and made his way to the front door. Inside, the crippled war veteran was humming a tune as he worked at the stove. Satisfied that no one else was inside, James swung the door open. It squeaked, and the cook looked up from his work in a casually indifferent manner.

"Figured someone would be along," he said in a scratchy voice.

"Is anyone else here?"

"Nope. Jest me."

"Where's Norris and his men?

"Now where do you think they are? They're with the cows."

"What's your name?"

"Lem Archer."

The big rancher walked over to Archer, towering over the smaller man by a full head and a half.

"What do you mean with the cows?" James asked.

"They're movin` the cows."

"To Tucson?"

"Yup."

"When did they leave?"

"This morning. I ain't seen Vic Norris that riled up before. You must be the one who got Villalobos."

"That's right," said James. He looked over the small ranch house with its one room for living and cooking and a second for sleeping. *Not much of a place to live*, he thought. *I'm glad I don't have to spend the night here.*

"Is that rifle the only weapon here?" Barringer asked, and pointed to the weapon leaning up against the wall.

"Yup."

Barringer moved to the door and motioned for Dave Forrester to join him. The cowboy entered and surveyed the bleak surroundings.

"Lem, my name is James Barringer, this is Dave Forrester. About five hundred cattle that Vic Norris rustled came from my ranch. I'm going to ask you some questions, and I want straight answers. Understood?" James stated in a strong voice.

"Yup."

"How many men does he have with him?"

"Fifteen."

"How long has he been using this as a headquarters for rustling?"

"About a year."

"How long have you been here?"

"About a year."

"Why did they leave you here?"

"I can't ride a horse any distance."

"Once they sell the cattle in Tucson, where would they head?"

"Don't know."

"Guess!" James ordered.

"Look, Mr. Barringer, if you're gonna kill me, you might as well git it over with. I ain't no rustler, I just work as a cook. Vic was the only one who would hire me. Not much call for a one-legged cook."

"How did you lose your leg?" Forrester asked.

"Shot off in the war. Couldn't get a job, so I became a cook. People don't like my food, so jobs are hard to come by."

There was a break in the tension as the two cowboys laughed.

"I'm not going to kill you, Lem," James said, grinning. "How many head of cattle do they have?"

"Between eight and nine hundred. When Villalobos disappeared, it put the fear of God into 'em. They decided to sell what they got and split. They'll be halfway to Tucson tomorrow."

"What are your plans when you leave here, Lem?"

"I was going to hitch up a couple of horses to that old wagon outside and head down to Sasabe on the Mex side of the border."

"Why are there so many horses in the corral?" Forrester asked.

"If they have to run, they would change horses here and head for the border."

Barringer and Forrester looked at one another.

"What do you have in the pot, Lem?" Forester asked.

"Beef stew."

"Let's see just how bad your cooking is," said James.

Lem limped around the kitchen, dished up two bowls, and placed them before the hungry cowboys. They both studied the combination of food in the bowls with suspicion. James took a taste and his eyes began to water.

"This stew is filled with peppers!"

"Right tasty, huh," said the cook.

"Is this meat beef?" Dave asked.

"You don't see no hogs on the property, do you?" Lem replied.

"Well, it's really soft and the peppers camouflage the taste. No offense meant," Forrester replied, smiling as he talked.

"None taken. It's been in the pot a few days."

"We used to call this mystery meat in the army, cooked so long you couldn't tell what you were eating," Dave said jokingly.

Lem gave him a dirty look. The cowboys spooned out as

many peppers as they could find and scraped everything off the chunks of meat. Their eyes still filled with tears as they ate. Lem pulled rolls out of the oven, and the men wolfed them down.

"Keep the water coming, Lem," said Dave Forrester.

"Where did you learn how to cook?" James asked.

"Taught myself."

James choked on a mouth full of food, trying to laugh and swallow at the same time. "Well, I tell you what, Lem. Tomorrow, hook up your wagon and head over to my ranch headquarters. Its due east of here. Tell my foreman, Silk Mathews, that I sent you. Have him put you up in the bunk house until I return. I'll find some place for you to work."

"As a cook?"

The two cowboys began laughing again. Just before dark, the men walked around the ranch and found several vantage points where Barringer's cowboys could fire at the corral area from concealed positions, shooting any returning outlaws.

"Kill them without any warning, Dave. They didn't give Cap or Silk any warning," he told Forrester. "Hang anyone left alive."

"It'll be my pleasure."

After night fall, the men returned to the Barringer camp site. Three men went with Forrester back to the ranch house. Barringer and the remaining group headed north towards Tucson, riding all night. By early light the next morning, they had located the cattle six miles to the west of the main trail. The pursuing column skirted the outlaws and continued north until the plains ended in low lying mountains. The flat area through the mountain foothills was about three hundred yards wide, used by all trail herds. Once the cattle were herded through this location, the rolling plains returned all the way to Tucson.

Barringer placed seven men behind rock outcroppings and had the remaining eight cowboys take similar positions on the other side of the wide trail. Their horses were removed to a nearby canyon.

"When you hear the first shot, start firing," he told the cowboys.

James found a vantage point behind a large boulder and waited for what he surmised would be a scout from the outlaw band. He and his men had not slept all night, but the cowboys were wide awake, anticipating the coming ambush.

CHAPTER 21

The dust cloud from the approaching herd became visible as cattle moved forward at a steady rate. The man riding point urged his horse forward and cautiously entered the ambush site. He was half a mile in front of the herd and wore a dark Stetson and a dark brown leather vest.

He continually turned his head from side to side, examining the rock formations on both sides of the trail. Twice he stopped and used binoculars, but the Barringer cowboys stayed hidden. He continued along the west side of the valley, turned, and began his return trip. James emerged from behind a boulder with his rifle aimed at the man's chest. The surprised outlaw's eyes widened.

"Get off your horse!" Barringer commanded.

The outlaw stared at James and then at his rifle. For a moment he seemed to consider raising his own rifle and firing, but the deadly look in Barringer's eyes dissuaded him. The outlaw dropped his rifle and slowly dismounted.

"Come over here!" James ordered. The scruffy looking rustler did as he was instructed. "What type of a sign are you to give back to the men driving the herd?" The outlaw hesitated. "One more chance, and then I'll kill you where you stand!"

"Wave my hat," he stammered.

"Take off your vest!"

The rustler did as he was told.

"Now, walk over to this boulder."

"You gonna let me live?"

"Sure. Now, sit down behind this outcropping."

As the outlaw started to sit James swung his rifle butt, striking him alongside the head. The rustler fell over moaning as Barringer used the rifle butt a second time, knocking him senseless, showing no mercy. He put on the man's hat and vest and mounted the outlaw's horse. James rode out into the center of the wide trail and turned towards the herd. A few minutes later he could make out two outlaws riding in front, one on each side of the herd. He took off the hat and waved, receiving a similar response in return from one of the rustlers. James turned the horse slowly and moved forward at a slow pace until he reached a large boulder, then dismounted and tied the horse to some bushes.

The herd was moving at a steady pace as it entered the wide trail between the foothills. James waited until the herd was substantially into the trap, then took careful aim and fired. His bullet knocked one of the lead men off his horse.

Pandemonium broke loose as the two lines of Barringer cowboys opened fire in unison. The herd bolted forward. Rustlers began firing back at the riflemen while trying to keep their mounts under control and out from under the stampeding cattle. Dust swirled, creating a large cloud, which made it difficult for the cowboys to see their adversaries. As the rustlers thundered by him, James shot two more outlaws off their horses.

In the center of the herd, the Barringer wranglers shot three more rustlers. The scene became chaotic as the huge cloud of dust made seeing nearly impossible. Three more outlaws were down, wounded, and attempted to crawl to the side of the herd to escape the hooves of the cattle. They were met with rapid fire and were shot dead.

The herd thundered along and two outlaws ducked forward on their horses, hoping they would not be noticed in the midst of the wild disorder. They made it past the ambush location and into the wide prairie, then split, with one heading west and the other east.

When the shooting began, three riders near the end of the herd had turned their horses and headed back in the direction from which they had come. A long distance shot was lucky enough to wound one of them.

Barringer let the cattle empty out into the grass covered plains, then cautiously came out from behind a boulder and walked towards the downed outlaws. Several cowboys joined him as one of the rustlers raised his revolver, trying to aim at the advancing men, but was killed before he could fire. Of the nine downed men, six were dead and three wounded. James dragged the unconscious scout from behind the rocks.

"What do you want us to do with them, Mr. Barringer?" one of his men asked.

"We'll hang them!" he responded. "Remember what happened to Cap."

A stand of mesquite and Palo Verde trees stood near a small creek that came down out of the low lying mountain range. Four rustlers were placed on horses, taken to the trees, and ropes put around their necks. At that moment, James recognized one of the twins, Jose Baca. He walked over to the young man and glared at him.

Baca appeared confused because of Barringer's change of clothing. He squinted at James. "Who are you?"

"I told you to find a different profession. You were never going to make it as a rustler."

Baca's angry eyes suddenly recognized Ricardo Montoya in Arizona cowboy clothing. "You son of a bitch!" he exclaimed.

One of the rustlers cried out, "For God's sake man, don't kill me!"

James looked at the four men one last time, no sympathy in his eyes, feeling nothing but hatred and the desire for revenge. Barringer walked behind the horses and sharply slapped each one on the rump. The horses bolted forward, yanking four outlaws out of their saddles. Rustlers cried out, began kicking wildly, struggling during the last spasms of life.

After the hanging was completed, the dead outlaws were tied over their saddles and the procession of bodies began its trip to Tucson. Six of Barringer's cowboys remained to round up the cattle and keep the herd together until the other cowhands returned. James sent three men on the trail of each of the outlaws who had escaped the ambush and were thought to be heading towards Tucson. James was confident that Dave Forrester and his men could handle the remaining outlaws who were retreating south back to the hideout for a change of horses and a change of scenery.

Near the end of the day, the long line of bodies on horses entered Tucson and headed for the town marshal's office. As the horses proceeded down the main street, men and women came out of the stores and began moving alongside the procession, shouting questions, yelling, creating an almost carnival-like atmosphere. James tried to ignore the gaggle of people, but the dead men were like magnets. The noise grew louder as people continually shouted to one another, attempting to guess what had occurred.

Town Marshal Jasper Sullivan came out of his office to determine what the commotion was all about. His mouth fell open when he saw the line of dead men tied to their horses, heading for his office.

Barringer pulled his mount to a halt in front of the lawman. "Marshal, these are rustlers led by an outlaw named Vic Norris. I'm James Barringer, in case you've forgotten. They took over five hundred head of cattle from the Barringer Ranch, and we went after them, ambushed them, and brought their bodies here. You might want to match up some of the faces to your wanted posters."

"You!" Sullivan exclaimed. "I haven't forgotten who you are. Every time I see you, someone dies. The town council won't like this, not one bit!"

Barringer dismounted and walked with Sullivan as he inspected the dead men.

"I see that you hung some of them."

"You are very observant, Marshal."

The crowd of people began to push one another in order to get better views. A fight broke out and Sullivan had to separate the men. He came rushing back to Barringer. "Can you take these dead men to the undertaker? It's up the block and to the left, then about two blocks on the right."

"Sure," said James. He motioned for his cowboys to start the procession moving again and they continued to the undertaker's office. A tall, gangly man with sunken cheeks, glittering eyes, and bad teeth greeted the procession with a smile and anticipation. "Tie them to the hitching rail, gentlemen," he said in a baritone voice.

Why do all undertakers look the same? Barringer mused. *They must be part of a brotherhood.*

203

The crowd continued to multiply as James walked away. He put his men up at the hotel, gave each of them ten dollars, and told the manager that food and drink at the hotel would be paid for by the Barringers. The hotel manager recognized James and looked skeptical, but agreed to Barringer's requests. James sent a rider to the herd to bring in the additional men, except for two guards, who would be replaced every four hours.

"Give me the largest and best room you have, and have a hot bath drawn."

"Right away, Mr. Barringer," the manager stated, and handed James a key to the Governor's Suite.

Barringer returned to Oro, mounted and took his favorite palomino to one of the local stables, then returned to the marshal's office. "Their leader, Vic Norris, got away," James told the marshal. "I'm sure you have a wanted poster on him."

Sullivan gave Barringer a look of disdain.

"How am I going to explain ten dead men to the town council? They are going to want answers. What do I do with ten bodies?" the marshal asked.

"Bury them. Look, Marshal, I've told you what happened. I'll give you some more details about the rustling and our ambushing the outlaws. That should be enough."

James spent the next ten minutes going over the details, starting with the shooting of Cap and Silk and ending with the ambush. Sullivan appeared to be somewhat appeased by the story, thinking it would be easier to explain now that he had a more complete chain of events in mind.

A Barringer cowboy, Mike Adams, came into the marshal's office. He had followed one of the two outlaws who had escaped the ambush and headed north. Adams told James that the trail led straight into Tucson. Barringer gave him spending money and sent him to the hotel. James thought for a moment and then shifted his gaze back to the marshal. "What saloon or other establishment might have the largest number of questionable customers in Tucson?"

Sullivan bristled. "We don't harbor criminals here."

"I don't mean to imply that. But outlaws and rustlers do tend to stick together. They feel more comfortable being with their own kind."

"I won't be a part of anything that means more killing," the marshal stated.

"See if you can find a wanted poster on Vic Norris. He has black hair, a black beard, and deep set eyes from what I've been told."

Reluctantly, Sullivan complied. He rustled through a number of posters and pulled one out that had Norris's name on it. The reward totaled five thousand dollars. Norris was wanted for murder and robbery in the New Mexico Territory.

"The Silver Bell," Sullivan said quietly without looking up. The men glanced at one another and Barringer shook his head in acknowledgement.

"It's owned by a man named Jesse Gates. Gates came here about a year ago and paid cash for the bar. Upstairs are several rooms, but he never advertises them for rent. Different men come and go. There's never any trouble there, but the type of people who frequent it are not church-goers," Sullivan emphasized.

Barringer thanked the marshal and went back to the hotel. He sent two men to the Silver Bell to drink and play cards and get a general feel for the environment. They came back two hours later and reported that the atmosphere was one of suspicion of all outsiders.

"Man! I never lost money that fast in my life. Every good

hand I had wasn't good enough," Mike Adams lamented.

"Did the men at the table ask questions?"

"They sure did. Where are you from? What brought you here? Who do you ride for? All those types of questions," said Adams. "There were a couple of whores upstairs making someone happy."

"Anything else?"

"Not really. A kid kept going up and down the stairs with food and drink. That's about it," Adams explained.

Barringer went back to the hotel, took a hot bath, and got dressed again. Following directions, he went to the Silver Bell and looked in as he walked by the swinging saloon doors. The bar clientele was beginning to thin out, but the card tables were full of men anxiously hoping to win. In general, the men were hard drinking, hard talking, and had ample money.

James walked down the alley between the bar and another building and looked in the back kitchen window. A young boy in his late teens was mopping the kitchen floor, but no one else was visible.

Barringer tapped on the window with a silver dollar, startling the boy, causing him to jerk his head up. James pointed to him and held up the silver dollar. The young man looked around, set down his mop, and came to the rear door. He unlocked it and peered out at Barringer.

"Take the dollar," James told him.

The boy appeared skeptical, but reached out and took the dollar.

"There are five more of these for you if you will give me a little information."

The door swung open. "What do you want to know?" he asked anxiously.

Barringer reached into his pocket and took out five more

silver dollars and tossed them up and down in his hand. The boy's eyes widened in anticipation.

"The man you were taking food and drinks to upstairs. Does he look like this man?" James asked him.

He showed him the drawing of Vic Norris that he had torn out of the wanted poster. The boy didn't appear to care where the drawing came from as he studied it closely.

"Yeah. That's him alright. Not a friendly guy. Even the whores don't like him."

"Which room is he in?"

The young man suddenly looked worried. "I'm not going to get in trouble, am I?" he asked in a worried tone of voice.

"It will be our secret," James said as he bounced the silver dollars in his hand. The boy's eyes followed every movement.

"He's in the last room on the right. The corner room," he revealed in wide-eyed anticipation.

James handed him the coins and smiled at the boy. The young man grinned at his good fortune, buried the coins in his pants pocket, and returned to his mop.

An outside deck ran around the second floor of the building, giving the guests a view of the commercial district in Tucson. Wrought iron railings installed in a diagonal pattern separated each room from one another.

Barringer walked slowly around the building looking for a fire escape or some other means to reach the second floor. There wasn't any. James walked around two other buildings before he found a ladder and carried it behind the buildings to the bar, placed it against the gambling house, and climbed to the second floor balcony. James tried the door but it was locked, as was the window. Barringer climbed over the wrought iron separation to the next room, finding the door was locked, but the window slid upward.

Silently he climbed in and made his way to the door, opened it, and looked out into the hallway just as a man came up the stairs from the saloon. He closed the door and waited. The door opened and a tall cowboy entered. Barringer used his revolver and smashed the man over the head, causing the cowboy to grunt and fall unconscious.

James moved quickly to the end room occupied by Vic Norris and heard a woman laugh. He quietly tried the handle but the door was locked from the inside. Barringer backed up one step, kicked the door knob hard, and the door flew inward. A naked whore was on the bed sitting on top of Norris. The outlaw reached for his revolver on the night stand and pulled the screaming whore down on top of him. Barringer fired at his hand, hitting him in the wrist.

Norris yelled, threw the whore off, and tried to grab the revolver with his other hand. The terrified woman began screaming hysterically and climbed down between the bed and the wall. James lunged at the outlaw, and they wrestled for control of his gun and ended up breaking through the door to the outside deck. The naked outlaw fought for his life as he and James traded blows, two large men pounding on each other, growling and grimacing.

A gunman rushed through the door and fired at Barringer just as the men whirled in a circle. The bullet struck Norris in the back of the head, and he gripped James tightly to keep from going down. The momentum of the two men propelled them backwards through the open window and against the iron balcony railing. It broke as Barringer thrust Norris away from him, pitching the naked outlaw's dead body through the railing into the street.

The outlaw in the doorway hesitated momentarily, distracted by the screaming whore, who was under the bed, and the fact that Norris was now in the street. James fired twice at the man's chest, driving the outlaw backward into the hallway, causing him to stumble down the corridor and fall head first down the stairs. The men rushing up the stairs were struck by the body, knocking them backwards to the floor of the saloon. The bar erupted in loud yells, but the sight of the dead gunman kept others from climbing the stairs. No one wanted to be next.

"Vic, can you hear me?" Jesse Gates cried out, standing at the base of the stairway.

A cowboy rushed into the saloon and yelled at Gates. "There's a naked dead man in the street! He came out of one of your windows."

"Goddamn it! All right, you men clear out. The marshal will be along soon," Gates growled.

The bar patrons holstered their guns and headed out the front door, most being wanted men who had no desire to talk to the marshal. Upstairs, James quickly reloaded his revolver, reached under the bed, grabbed the hysterical woman by the arm, and pulled her out. He took the prostitute to the door and pushed her out into the hallway. *Anything to stop that screaming*, he thought.

***

Gates stepped out in the street as men carrying lanterns were rushing to view the dead man in the evening's darkness. Tucson Town Marshal Jasper Sullivan came running up to the bar. "Who's the dead man?" Sullivan asked loudly.

"He told me his name was Robert Simpson," Gates responded. "He paid in cash for everything."

"I warned you about running a clean establishment here!"

"You haven't had any trouble from me," Gates contended.

"Who shot him?"

"The man's still upstairs."

Sullivan turned to walk into the saloon just as Barringer came out the front door, revolver in hand.

"Barringer!" Sullivan yelled. "Every time I see you, someone is dead! This is the second time you've thrown a man out of a second story window."

"It didn't exactly happen that way. That dead man is Vic Norris, head of the rustlers, shot by the cowboy lying dead on the stairs inside."

"There's another dead man!" Sullivan exclaimed. He looked from Barringer to Gates, eyes wide, doubt and disbelief etched on his face. "Get a blanket to cover this body, Gates. We can't have a naked dead man in the street."

Norris's body was covered while James explained what had occurred and how the shootings had transpired. An anguished marshal listened, but his face was twisted with anger. "What am I going to tell the town council? They're adamant that violence be curtailed in Tucson. This isn't Tombstone, where someone is killed every day."

"Tell them that the five thousand dollar reward for Vic Norris is going to whatever Tucson charity they choose," Barringer said in a calm voice.

"Really?"

"Sure. You'll be a hero."

Sullivan thought for a moment. *Well, that might work,* he reasoned. "Come over to my office in the morning. I'll be involved with a lot of paperwork over…this," Sullivan noted.

CHAPTER 22

Dave Forrester had stationed his men at three locations around the corral in case any outlaws made it back to the ranch. The following morning his lookout came riding in at full gallop. "It looks like three men are coming in. One of them is wounded, from the way he's bent over the saddle," the cowboy told Forrester. Dave signaled his men to take cover.

Five minutes later the rustlers appeared and rode directly to the corral, horses lathered and near collapse. As soon as the rustlers dismounted, they were fired at from three locations. The wounded outlaw was shot through the back and head and was dead before he hit the ground. A second outlaw ran to the ranch house and was shot in the leg as he dove inside. The third rustler also made it to the ranch house, untouched by bullets striking near him. Both men quickly returned fire but hit no one.

"Come out of there, or we'll burn you out!" Forrester yelled.

"Screw you!" came the reply.

Forrester nodded to one of the cowboys. "Take those two lanterns around back, light them, and throw them up on the roof," he ordered. A few minutes later, the cowboy hurled the lanterns onto the wood shake roof. The fire spread quickly, and within minutes the entire top of the ranch house was ablaze.

Smoke came out of the front window and door, and the two rustlers were forced to run outside, coughing and firing their revolvers. The first man ran quickly towards the bunkhouse, bullets whizzing around him, but none found their mark until Forrester took careful aim and shot him through the middle of the back, killing him.

Last out the door was the third outlaw with the wounded leg, hobbling as fast as possible. The cowboys peppered him with rifle shots, knocking him to the ground. Although down, he continued to crawl towards the bunkhouse, firing continuously, striking one of Barringer's men in the arm before he ran out of ammunition. Forrester walked up to him and put a bullet through his head.

Dave set fire to the bunkhouse, and it quickly went up in flames. The cowboys buried the dead outlaws, collected the horses, and the procession began its return trip to the ranch.

**

James and his men began herding nearly seven hundred cattle into corrals next to the railroad siding outside of town. Two cattle buyers came up to Barringer. "Are you Norris?" one of the buyers asked.

"I'm James Barringer. Norris is dead. He and his men were rustling my cattle and stock from several other ranches south of here. Didn't you hear about the dead bodies being brought into Tucson?"

"Yeah, but no one put names on them," said a buyer with tawny, honey colored eyes.

"I killed Norris last night."

212

"We all heard about that," exclaimed the buyer named Cal Runyan. "I guess we'll deal with you since Norris is dead." Runyan was of medium height with light brown hair down to his shoulders and a matching moustache and goatee.

"You're not too careful who you buy from," James commented.

"Listen, Mr. Barringer, when cattle come in, they have many brands on them. Sometimes there are representatives from each ranch, and sometimes just one man is selling," he responded matter-of-factly. "We've got no way of verifying where they came from."

James gave him a questioning look and changed the subject. "How much are you offering per head?"

"Seventeen dollars per head."

"I think we'll wait and talk with some other buyers. I think we can get twenty-two dollars per head."

The two buyers looked at each other, then Runyan turned his attention back to James and held out his hand. "Twenty-two dollars per head it is," said the cattle buyer.

They shook hands and James told one of his cowhands to check the brands as they were loaded. "If they have different brands, count how many there are. I'll pay the other ranchers for their stock," he told the Barringer cowboy. By the end of the day, James had concluded his business. Nearly one hundred and fifty cattle were owned by other ranchers, so the Barringer Ranch had netted just over twelve thousand dollars.

James was tired when he reached the hotel. A hot bath was waiting for him, and he soaked in the water for half an hour, dried himself off, and was reaching for his clothes when there was a knock at the door. He wrapped a towel around his waist, pulled his revolver from its holster, and opened the door.

Marshal Jasper Sullivan stood there with a short, fat businessman dressed in a dark suit. The little man's eyes were mere slits, and his jowls hung down below his chin, covering the upper portion of his string tie. His eyes darted up and down Barringer, and he was not quite able to hide his distaste for the tall cowboy.

"Sorry to bother you so late," said Sullivan. "But there's some unfinished business we need to resolve before you leave town."

Barringer motioned for them to come inside. "What is it?"

"I'd like you to meet Mayor Horatio Pillpot."

The two men shook hands.

"You see, it's this way, Mr. Barringer. The five thousand dollar reward for Vic Norris can't be paid directly to the city fathers because we didn't have anything to do with catching him," the mayor said in a low, guttural voice.

Pillpot was nearly two heads shorter than Barringer, and his eyes constantly moved up and down James's big torso, with his gaze stopping momentarily at numerous battle scars spread over Barringer's body. James could feel the mayor's intense dislike.

"Give me a second to get my clothes on," said Barringer as he walked back into the bathroom, and came out a few minutes later fully dressed.

"Is it still your intent to give the money to the town council for charity purposes?" Pillpot asked.

"Yes."

"Then we'll need you to sign the money over to the town council," he said matter-of-factly.

"All right, I'll be happy to do that."

Pillpot pulled a sheet of paper from his inside coat pocket and handed it to Barringer. James read it, and his eyes narrowed. "This says I'm signing it over to you, not to the town council."

Sullivan had a pained expression on his face, and he kept his eyes focused on the floor.

"I assure you, the town council will do anything I desire," Pillpot stated.

"Are you comfortable with this, Marshal?"

Sullivan suddenly had a frightened look in his eyes. "Yes."

"Give me a pen."

Barringer signed his name, but added a sentence that said, "This agreement must be approved by the town council before the money is released to Mayor Pillpot."

The mayor grabbed the paper and hurriedly read the new verbiage. "I object to this, Mr. Barringer! It makes me think that you don't trust me."

"It's not that I don't trust you. I don't know you."

"I'm the mayor. Everyone trusts me!" Pillpot proclaimed.

The marshal began breathing hard and perspiring. Pillpot's face turned red.

"Take it or leave it, Mayor," James emphasized.

Clutching the paper, the mayor turned and left the room.

"I hope I never have to see you again," the marshal said in a low voice as he departed, anger etched on his face. Barringer smiled as he closed the door. Two hours later the mayor returned with a proclamation signed by the other council members, authorizing the money to be turned over to Pillpot.

The following morning James and the cowhands headed south, and reached the Barringer Ranch on the evening of the second day. Silk and Dave were summoned to Victoria's office, and Barringer related the details of the ambush outside of Tucson. Forrester did the same concerning the killing of the remaining outlaws at their ranch headquarters and the demolition of the buildings.

"How many do you think got away?" Silk asked.

"One or two at most. It's hard to say, exactly."

Victoria was pleased. "Now we can discuss your next venture, which I assume is going back to Hermosillo to collect your bride to be."

"Christina's marriage to Miguel Soto is scheduled in about a week," James noted.

"My leg is a lot better. Do you want me to go with you?" Silk asked.

"No. If I took men with me, it would draw attention immediately. I'll slip into town and talk with our lawyer, Alfredo Garcia, and get a feel for things."

They chatted and discussed ranch business for the next hour before James went to bed.

***

Barringer reached The Crossing about dinner time the following day and found Paco in the stables.

"Chameleon! It is good to see you. Your clothes are ready," the smiling stable owner stated.

"You look surprisingly fit. It's good to see you back on your feet again."

The men went to the small cantina and ate dinner. James Barringer had changed into Mexican clothing and now had become Ricardo Montoya. He told Paco about the rustlers, the ambush, and the killing of most of the outlaws.

"Jose Baca left here as soon as he was able to ride," said Flores. "Was he one of them?" Their eyes met and held, and Ricardo nodded his head. Paco grimaced, and a hurt look came over his face.

"He died in the fighting," Montoya said, not wanting to tell his friend that he hung Baca.

216

"His father, Marcos, and I have become good friends. Marcos was a great help in keeping the stable operating properly while I recovered. I know he felt terrible when his son left this last time."

"Jose chose the wrong road."

Paco shook his head from side to side. "You know, they all want to make easy money."

"What about the other son, Pepe?"

"He's still here. You put the fear of God into him. I think he will stay honest."

"Do you want me to tell Marcos?" Ricardo asked.

"No. I'll do it. Is there any chance of getting his body back for burial?"

"The dead outlaws were taken to Tucson and buried there. There aren't any names on the graves."

"Let's have another drink," Paco said, and sighed. For the next hour, they talked about the twists and turns that life takes, expectations, triumphs, and tragedies.

"Do you have your heart set on marrying that woman?"

"Yes. She's always on my mind. If she turns me down, I don't know what I'll do."

"You have it bad. The love bug bit you hard." The men laughed and Paco continued to kid Ricardo about his star crossed love life.

***

Ricardo was up early the next morning, saddled a black stallion, said goodbye to Paco, and set off on the trail to Hermosillo. He arrived in the bustling cattle and mining community late that afternoon, circumvented the center of the town, and stayed near the outskirts until dark, when he arrived at Alfredo Garcia's home. Ricardo saw that the home was ablaze with lights and recognized that Garcia was entertaining. About ten o'clock in the evening, the carriages began leaving for the short ride into the city. Ricardo walked up to the home and looked into various windows until he spotted Garcia in his office giving final instructions to the staff members. As the house maids and butlers filed out, Montoya tapped on the window, startling Garcia, whose head jerked up. The lawyer looked at the window and his mouth dropped open as he recognized Ricardo. Garcia left the office and walked around to a side entrance, motioning for Montoya to join him. They entered a back room and the lawyer closed the door.

"What in God's name are you doing here?" asked the amazed attorney.

"I came to see Christina."

"She's under guard. The whole group came here last night for dinner, and there were a dozen bodyguards stationed around this entire house. You'll be shot on sight if anyone sees you."

The men sat down and Alfredo opened a side bar and poured brandy for them. He left the room for a moment and told the staff that he did not want to be disturbed.

"I believe that she will break the engagement, if I ask her to, and I intend to do that."

"Don't fool yourself, Ricardo. They will kill anyone who would try to stop this marriage."

"I'll be careful. Is she still staying at the hotel?"

"Yes. I just finished formulating the contracts for the two families over who will invest, how much will be invested, how the profits are to be divided, and formation of an annual review committee. The contracts are voluminous and cover every aspect of the partnership between the Sotos and the Aragons."

"I hope I won't do anything to upset all the work you've put in," said Ricardo.

Garcia laughed. "I've already been paid. As soon as they reviewed and approved the paperwork my job was done, and I was very well paid. If it were to fall apart, I've still made my money."

"Tell me about Christina. How did she act when she was here for dinner?"

"She looks as beautiful as ever, but she was quiet and very reserved. I can tell that she is not in favor of the marriage. She and Miguel Soto never even looked at one another."

"I'm relieved to hear that. Does the little butler or servant still follow Soto around?

"Yes, he was here, but stayed outside with the bodyguards. I remember what you told me. Does Christina know?"

"I told her and she believed me, but at that point she was still willing to go through with the wedding. It wasn't until the Aragons and Soto were leaving his rancho that she told me to come back for her. She'd changed her mind."

"What did happen involving the Apache raid and the demolishing of Aragon's hacienda and mine? Don Ramon's version is most improbable," Garcia emphasized.

Montoya recounted the events from the moment he warned them about the impending attack to paying Aragon ten thousand dollars to leave the peons at the new rancho.

"I knew the story was fiction! He claimed that you destroyed his rancho while he was fighting the Apaches and the army made you pay ten thousand dollars in restitution. He said criminal charges will be brought against you."

Ricardo began laughing and Garcia joined him.

"The man lives in a fantasy world. He doesn't grasp the realities of life when it comes to telling the truth," Ricardo said.

"You know, Ricardo, I entertain all the time, and it's very seldom that I have a client like Don Ramon. You can't believe a word he says, yet Christina's father and the Soto family are going to contribute more than a hundred thousand dollars to his mining enterprises. And that's just for starters."

"There are many successful mines in the region," Montoya noted.

"I don't think his is one of them. The brokers who buy gold from the mines tell me that his transactions are small. He is barely able to pay his bills, and the banks continue to extend him loans."

"Are you sure about that?" Ricardo asked.

"I'm sure. My law firm does most of the contractual paperwork for businesses in the community. These business leaders confide in me and relay all the gossip they hear. I think Don Ramon is nearly broke."

CHAPTER 23

Ricardo walked the streets around the Hermosillo Hotel, wearing white peon's clothing and a multi-colored poncho. He paid a hotel employee and learned Christina and her aunt were in a large suite complete with living room, two bedrooms, two bathrooms, and a formal dining room. He continuously roamed the streets, and for the sixth time that night Montoya looked up at suite 317 at the corner of the building, and finally saw her step out onto the balcony. The moon was full and illuminated her cream-colored silk dress and light complexion. Christina became part of the ornate exterior of the hotel, beautiful and untouchable. Montoya came out of the shadows and moved to the edge of the boardwalk across the street. Light shining through the windows from the building behind him outlined his silhouette as he removed his dark sombrero, illuminating his face as he stared upward.

***

Christina let her eyes wander around the lighted city below her, and then her gaze dropped to the street directly below. She glanced at the man standing on the boardwalk, thinking he looked familiar. Suddenly she moved forward and gripped the wrought iron railing with both hands, her facial features frozen and her eyes wide as she stared at Ricardo, recognizing him in spite of the peon's clothing he was wearing.

Ricardo momentarily stepped back into the shadows and replaced his sombrero as two guards walked out of the hotel, looked up and down the street, and began an easy stroll down to the end of the block. Montoya stepped back into the moonlight, stuck his right arm into the air, and waved once. Their eyes met and held as seconds passed, neither one wanting to look away, the power of unspoken love gripping them tightly. Finally, fear of being discovered made Ricardo begin a leisurely stroll away from the hotel.

He's come back, she thought. *He's come back for me*! Christina closed her eyes and bowed her head slightly as he disappeared from view. Tears rolled down her cheeks as emotions took over, hope replacing sinister frustrations and pessimism.

***

Ricardo walked around the entire block and ended up behind the hotel at the employee's entrance. He waited until a young woman came out, caught up with her, and handed her a leather pouch filled with coins.

The woman was startled and looked confused. "I'm not that kind of woman," she told the tall peon.

"The money's not for that. I want you to do me a favor and take a note to the woman in Suite 317. If you are successful and bring a note back to me, I will double this amount of money."

She studied him for a moment. "That suite is under heavy guard. No one can get in or out of those rooms without authorization."

"Do you clean it?"

"Yes. I've been in there on several occasions to change sheets and clean the bathrooms, windows, and floors. But we are always watched by the guards."

"I want you to give this note to Christina Aragon, but don't let her aunt see you do it. Can you try?"

The young, black-haired woman looked up at Ricardo. "You're him, aren't you? You're the one they talk about, the one they're afraid of!"

"Yes."

"I'll try. I'll switch with one of the other women tomorrow morning. I think the cleaning crew goes in at ten o'clock," she told him, and took the folded note.

"I would greatly appreciate it. I'll wait here at the rear of the hotel for you tomorrow."

"There are many men trying to keep you away from Senorita Aragon. She is always polite to the hotel workers, but she seems very sad."

"I'll try to put a smile on her face," Ricardo said, and grinned.

"A word of warning," she observed.

"What is it?"

"Your eyes are not the eyes of a peon. Don't look people directly in the eyes when you pass them. You must look down."

Montoya thought for a moment. "I understand," he replied.

Ricardo walked to a small hotel two blocks away and went to his room on the main floor. Seated in a chair by the window, he looked out into the moonlit street, watching people walk by. A young man and woman stopped and kissed. *I would give anything to be with her*, he thought.

***

The following morning the young hotel worker, Carmen Diaz, joined the cleaning crew that headed to Christina's suite.

Two guards at the front door carefully looked over the men in the cleaning group, and satisfied that no one posed a threat, the door was opened and the workers went in. No one was in the suite, much to Carmen's disappointment. The crew went about the cleaning process in a business-like manner, and were just completing the work when Christina and Aunt Olivia returned.

"What was that waiter thinking of, bringing me runny eggs? Well, they haven't heard the last of it from me," Olivia complained.

Christina was barely listening, her mind fixed on Ricardo, her body just going through the motions. *He's really here*, she thought. *He'll find some way for us to be together, I know he will.*

Carmen approached Christina, bumped her arm, and thrust the note into her hand. The two women looked into each others eyes, and Christina instinctively knew who the note was from. They passed one another without exchanging a word, and Christina went into the bathroom and closed the door.

She unfolded the note, which said, *Send someone you can trust to the Hernandez Hotel, room 101. I love you.*

Christina's heart was pounding as she wrote on the bottom of the note. *I will send someone. Please be careful. I love you, too.* She walked into the living room, casually passing Carmen, and slipped the note into her apron pocket. Carmen was one of the first to leave the suite, and quickly went to the back of the hotel and walked across the street to where Ricardo was waiting. She exchanged the note for additional money.

"I can get more messages to her," she told Ricardo.

***

After lunch Christina returned to the room and steered her aunt to a brocade couch in the comfortable living room.

"Aunt Olivia, I have a question for you."

The older woman looked over at her niece. "What is it?"

"Have you ever been in love?"

Olivia looked stunned and didn't answer.

Christina repeated the question. "Have you ever been in love?"

"Of course. I was married to my husband for twenty years before he died."

"Did you love him?" she asked quietly, her eyes never leaving her aunt's face.

Olivia hesitated, her eyes dropped to the floor, and she began breathing heavily. "We got along well at the beginning, but grew apart."

"You also lived apart, as I remember."

Olivia suddenly had a pained expression on her face as her mouth dropped open and her eyes widened. "It was an arranged marriage. We weren't well suited for one another."

"Were you ever in love before the marriage? I mean, with another man?"

That question brought tears to Olivia's eyes and she let out an agonized whimper. Victoria continued to stare at her aunt, waiting for an answer, not allowing her to escape the trap.

Suddenly, Olivia blurted out, "I was very much in love with Hector Gonzales, the son of a store owner, and he loved me. My parents would not let me marry him because he did not have social status. I was forbidden to see him again. Hector joined the Spanish army and was killed in one of those stupid wars between the countries." The older lady began crying. "He would be alive today if it weren't for me. I think about him all the time. He was the only man I ever loved."

Victoria put her arms around her sobbing aunt. After a

few moments, she put her hands on her aunt's shoulders and looked into her eyes. "Would you condemn me to that same type of loveless marriage?"

"Oh, God! Why are you doing this to me?" Olivia babbled. Her eyes contained an almost grief-stricken look as she began weeping, emitting short, gasping breaths.

"Would you condemn me, Aunt Olivia?"

Olivia's eyes were red-rimmed and filled with tears. She suddenly seized the strength to lash out at the demons that had haunted her all these years. "No!" she exclaimed. "No, don't go through with it if you feel that way. Day by day, year by year, you will begin to hate him and hate yourself. I don't even recognize the woman I used to be. You are the only person I love."

"I love you, too, Aunt Olivia."

Olivia clutched her niece in her arms and was shaking as she cried.

"Will you help me?" Victoria said quietly.

Olivia tried unsuccessfully to quench her tears. "I will help you in any way I can," she sniffled.

"I'm deeply in love with Ricardo Montoya."

Olivia's red rimmed eyes opened wide and she quickly sat up. "Oh! He's a hard man. You'd be better off with a polite, well-bred member of the aristocracy."

Christina gently took hold of her aunt's hands. "Isn't that what your parents told you?"

Olivia's face became distorted, an expression of intense pain clouded her features, and she let out an animal-like cry as she burst out crying again.

***

An hour later, Aunt Olivia went out the front door of the hotel and headed down the street with two bodyguards in attendance. The short lady had a large parasol to deflect the sun's rays, and she whirled it continuously above her head. She made a left turn and walked towards a woman's dress shop in the next block. Whirling around, she fixed the bodyguards with a hawk-like, predatory gaze. "You men can go into the bar, there," she said, and pointed to a nearby cantina. "When I'm finished, you can carry my packages back to the hotel."

"Our orders are to accompany you everywhere," said one of the men.

"Do as I have instructed, or I will go back to the hotel and complain about your incompetence and unwillingness to assist me!" she hissed.

One vaquero looked at the other and both men headed for the bar. "She is one mean bitch!" a tall bodyguard said to his short companion.

A satisfied smile settled on her face as she reached the dress shop, made a detour to the left, and walked to the small hotel where Ricardo was staying. She went by the desk and over to the corridor that led to Montoya's room.

"May I help you, madam?" a short, skinny clerk asked.

Olivia whirled around, a look of fury on her face. "Don't bother me, young man," she said loudly.

The clerk dropped his gaze to the desk, deciding to remain quiet. She arrived at Ricardo's room and knocked quietly on the door. Ricardo walked to the door, opened it, and the two adversaries stood there staring at one another. Ricardo looked up and down the corridor, and then motioned for her to come inside.

"I never expected to see you here."

"I never expected to be here." She walked over to the one chair in the room and sat down.

Ricardo was amazed. *What is she doing here?* he thought.

"Christina convinced me that the marriage is wrong for her. She doesn't love Miguel. I, myself, was in a loveless marriage for many years. I'm here to offer my help in getting Christina out of that marriage. Do you want me to speak with Miguel about cancelling tomorrow's ceremony?"

Ricardo's face hardened as he stood over the elderly woman. "No. There's only one way the Sotos and the Aragons would cancel that marriage, and it would be if I put a bullet between Miguel's eyes."

"Oh!" she said. "Well, what do you want me to do?"

"With your assistance, it will be much easier to accomplish what I have in mind. Here's the plan and how you can help Christina."

When he was finished, she looked at Ricardo with new respect. "A lot of things would have to happen quickly for this to work."

"If you have a better idea, I'm listening."

Olivia thought for a moment. "No, I don't. I never liked you, but Christina is madly in love with you, so I'll do as you ask."

Ricardo's eyes lit up and he smiled. "This could be the beginning of a terrific relationship," he said facetiously.

CHAPTER 24

The All Saints Church had a long history dating back seventy years, but was too small to accommodate all families invited to the wedding, so the ceremony was to be conducted on a raised platform in front of the church. The wedding reception area was situated in a large half circle beyond the raised platform, in order to give all who attended good views of the ceremony.

Large open sided tents were set up in a half circle around the front of the legendary church. Piñatas hung from the centers of the tents, while white wedding banners were strung across the front of the church and from sides of the tents. Multi-colored paper flags adorned the tables, and the entire wedding reception area was ablaze with different colors. Lavish spreads of food were laid out on tables behind the platform. Musicians were playing soft pieces up to the point when the prospective bride and groom mounted the platform, then there was silence. Father Jose Verdugo moved towards the pair and raised his hand in preparation for prayer.

Christina was dressed in a traditional white silk wedding dress with a mantilla veil, her expression solemn. Miguel

Soto wore a black silk suit with bolero jacket and tight fitting pants accented with silver clasps up the sides of the legs. His black hair, black moustache, and goatee gave him the look of a Mexican nobleman.

The first of the firecracker bombs exploded to the right of the platform, followed by four others, one after another, around the periphery of the reception area. The blasts resembled rifle fire, creating intense fear among the wedding viewers. Pandemonium broke loose, and confusion and disorder reigned as people ran in every direction, screaming, thinking they were being attacked. Frightened men and women bumped into each other as they ran; food and drink were splattered and spilled everywhere. Miguel Soto jumped off the platform and rolled underneath, seeking safety from whoever was firing.

***

On cue, Christina ran into the church and towards the back, where she quickly took off her dress and put on a leather riding outfit. Two more of the firecracker bombs were detonated as she and Ricardo mounted horses at the rear of the church and rode away.

***

People continued to scream and yell as wild disorder prevailed. No one was injured, but the reception area was a shambles of knocked over tents, food scattered over the ground, and people literally running around in circles. The boys responsible for the cherry bomb attack were on the run away from the church, laughing as they made their escape. They had been well paid for the exercise, and had timed it perfectly.

Don Ramon climbed out from under a table and wiped the dust and dirt from his clothing. "An outrage! Find out who did this! Someone will pay for this violent act!" Miguel Soto rolled out from under the platform once he was sure no more explosions were taking place. "This was a sick joke. I will kill whoever was responsible," Soto vowed, his eyes reflecting fury.

Father Jose Verdugo was in shock, sitting on the raised platform, eyes wide and face white. Bodyguards were running around, guns drawn, trying to locate the attackers. It was ten minutes before the wedding participants began returning to the church.

"There's nothing more we can do today," Soto told Aragon. "We'll try again tomorrow if the priest is willing. I'll get Christina, and we can head back to the hotel. Where is she?" he said, looking around.

The two men searched for Christina among the ruins of the wedding decorations, tables and tents, but she was nowhere to be found. Soto suddenly realized the truth, screamed with anguish, and rushed into the church. He ran to the rear and searched the rooms, releasing an animal-like cry upon locating the wedding dress. Soto ran outside at the rear of the church and then back to the front.

"She's gone!" he yelled at Aragon.

"Gone! What do you mean, gone?" the fat don replied in a shrill voice.

"Her wedding dress is in the back room. This was a ruse, a trick, and I know Ricardo Montoya was behind this abomination."

"Oh, no!" Don Ramon screeched. "Where did they go?"

"North, of course. North to the Arizona Territory. But we can run them down," Soto declared. He gathered his bodyguards and sent them riding north on the only trail to Arizona.

"Kill both of them," he ordered.

"What are you saying?" an alarmed Don Ramon demanded.

"I have been humiliated in front of my family and my friends. The only way I can gather my honor back is to kill them both. Without respect from my friends, I have nothing, and they've made a gigantic fool out of me!" he yelled.

Aragon's eyes were wide. He attempted to sit down on one of the folding chairs, but a partially broken leg gave way and he tumbled on to the ground. "I'm ruined," he growled.

Olivia Aragon knew the explosions were coming, but still was shocked by the loud noises. She sat down at one of the few tables that was still standing in the reception area, a smile on her face. She thought about her one true love, Hector Gonzales, believing she had struck a blow, avenging his needless death. "I think I'll be going back to Spain," she said to herself. "Go with God, Christina. Go with the one you love."

The man and woman riding horses northward were Jaime and Guadalupe Mendoza, recruited by Ricardo to leave a false trail. They passed through two small communities along the road and continued until they were about ten miles north of Hermosillo. Guadalupe changed from a leather riding outfit into a white cotton dress as her husband changed into a peon's cotton shirt and pants. At a prescribed location he hooked up one of the horses to a small cart filled with fire wood, and he and his wife departed back the way they had come from Hermosillo.

Jaime continued for another few miles until he came to a corral and switched the horse for a mule. The Mendozas passed small groups of people coming from the city, and once in a while would stop to chat. Then they encountered eight horsemen galloping northward. Soto's men stopped and the leader asked if there were a man and woman on horseback ahead. Jaime said yes, he had passed a man and woman. A bodyguard described Montoya, and he shook his head yes. "That could be him," he replied.

As the armed gunmen entered a small community two hours later, their horses were exhausted, so they rested the animals and ate an early dinner. To their surprise, no one in the small community had seen a man and woman matching the description of Ricardo and Christina. Their leader decided they should return to Hermosillo for further instructions.

Soto accepted the news in an insolent, pompous manner, flying into a rage, berating the gunmen for incompetence and their inability to follow a simple trail. After his initial outburst, Soto sat down in his hotel room and reviewed a map of the Mexican states of Sonora and Chihuahua. From Hermosillo, a second trail led northeast to Agua Prieta on the Arizona border, and a third went directly east to Chihuahua and then north to Ciudad Juarez and El Paso. The following morning, Soto sent four men on the northeast trail to Agua Prieta, and another four men on the Chihuahua trail with orders to question everyone they met about seeing a man and woman on horseback heading away from Hermosillo.

The men following the Agua Prieta trail found no one who had seen the pair. The gunmen following the Chihuahua trail learned that a carriage had passed along the route, containing a man and woman matching the description of Ricardo and Christina. One of the bodyguards rode back to Hermosillo and reported the news to Soto, who quickly assembled ten men for the three day trip to Chihuahua. They were one day behind.

***

"I feel like a fugitive," Christina jokingly told Ricardo.

Ricardo had his arms wrapped around her and an exhilarating feeling swept over him. He hardly noticed the bumping of the coach. The first night was spent camping out under the stars, but intimacy was not to be because of the coach driver. The second night they spent in Ciudad Guerrero, which had a small hotel/cantina, and the pair got very little sleep.

When they entered the outskirts of Chihuahua, Christina and Ricardo reverted back to using their horses. The carriage was parked inside a hay barn, and the well-paid driver was told to wait four days before beginning the return trip. A thriving economic center in northern Mexico, the city was a trade center for cattle and agricultural products and projected an energetic, vigorous feel as business and commerce flourished. Carriages and mounted men filled the streets, and the boardwalks held an unending number of men, women, and children moving from one location to another.

People stared at the pair as they rode down the street towards the center of Chihuahua. Christina's dark hair curled around her shoulders as she rode her horse in the traditional style, not side saddle. Every man's eyes instinctively moved to her curvaceous body in a tight-fitting leather riding outfit. Ricardo's muscular body, handsome face, and curly dark hair were accented by his well tailored calf skin outfit and sombrero, adorned with gold embroidery. Women on the boardwalk cast admiring looks and smiles at Montoya.

Ricardo asked directions to Manuel Verdugo's new mercantile store, where the merchandise included everything from women's dresses and fabrics to men's clothing, guns, saddles, and a full line of hardware, implements, and tools. Montoya had frequently purchased supplies from Verdugo when he was segundo on the Salazar rancho.

They dismounted in front of the store, and as they entered, Manuel walked over to them, grabbed Ricardo's hand, and shook it vigorously. "It's good to see you, my friend," Verdugo said.

"It's been a long time, I know. I'd like you to meet Christina Aragon, my fiancée."

Manuel was impressed. "It is my pleasure, Miss Aragon," he said, beaming.

Christina smiled. "Thank you. I love that dress you have in the window."

"It's my wife's selection. She handles the entire women's stock."

After they chatted for a few minutes, Christina excused herself and walked to the women's section.

"This store is three times the size of your old one," Ricardo noted.

"Business has been good. Chihuahua is the hub of commerce in northern Mexico. It draws families like flowers draw bees."

"I need to talk with you in private," Ricardo said quietly.

Manuel pointed to a side door. "Let's go into my office."

Ricardo told Christina where he would be and asked her to join them when she finished shopping. The men sat down at a small, round table in front of Verdugo's desk.

Montoya explained the very complicated situation involving Christina, her previous engagement to Miguel Soto, escaping with her from the altar, and their flight to Chihuahua.

Verdugo, a tall, dignified man with a neatly trimmed moustache and long sideburns, sat back in his chair and exhaled loudly, a look of disbelief on his face. "You're in a lot of trouble!"

"I'm sure Soto and his gunmen are after us. I need your

advice on how to proceed north to Ciudad Juarez without getting caught. I know we could stay in Chihuahua for a few days, but we are both anxious to leave Mexico and begin a new life."

"The stage coach left yesterday for Ciudad Juarez. It runs every three days, but taking it isn't a good idea. Too many people would remember the two of you taking the stage coach," Manuel pointed out.

"By now, Soto has determined that we didn't take trails leading north, and he probably is a day or less behind us," Ricardo surmised.

Verdugo thought for a moment. "Is it too long a trip for Christina to ride a horse?"

"Yes, it would be too hard on her."

They discussed various options until Christina came to the office and joined them. Ricardo put his arm around Christina and smiled. "There's a favor you could do for us, Manuel."

"Name it."

"Can you arrange for us to get married now before we leave?"

Manuel's eyes opened wide. "Right now?"

"Yes!" Christina emphasized. "I don't want to be left at the altar again." They laughed, and Verdugo congratulated them.

The store owner took them to a small church at the end of the street frequented by peons, vaqueros, and their families. Father Dominic Castro came out from a room at the rear, bible in hand, alerted by Verdugo about the request for an impromptu marriage without frills. The priest was bald, had a heavily lined face, and wore a brown robe with a cord around his waist. The thin padre looked at the couple in front of him and was surprised. The woman was beautiful and wore a new dress from Manuel's store. Her betrothed was very tall and dressed in fine leather clothing that only a don could afford.

"These are humble surroundings," he explained in an almost apologetic manner. "Perhaps you would be more comfortable in the large cathedral that the city leaders frequent on the other side of Chihuahua?"

"Your church will be fine, Father," Christina responded in a soft, friendly voice. "We appreciate you performing the ceremony on such short notice."

Verdugo had brought a ring, which he gave to Ricardo. The wedding ceremony was short and to the point, and Ricardo put the ring on Christina's finger and kissed her out of sequence.

"I now pronounce you man and wife," said Father Castro.

He kissed her again and was suddenly overcome by the enormity of the simple ceremony, feeling confused, terrified, and extremely happy. Montoya simultaneously experienced feelings of deep respect, love, and awe for his new wife as he looked into her eyes. Ricardo, the quick decision maker and assertive leader of men, appeared bewildered, not knowing what to do.

She saw an emotional man in front of her. "Ricardo, I'm so happy to be married to you," she said with a cheerful smile. "Everything will be fine, dear." Christina put her hands around Ricardo's neck, pulled his head down, and kissed him hard on the mouth. Ricardo came out of his trance and returned the kiss.

Everyone thanked Father Castro. As they were preparing to leave, Ricardo pulled a purse filled with gold coins from his pocket and handed it to the priest. "I hope you and your parish can use this," said Montoya. The priest was shocked, took Ricardo's hand, and told him that God worked in mysterious ways.

Verdugo and Montoya had earlier decided that a brief stay under the Arriaga Rim north of Chihuahua would be best solution to their short term problem.

"There's still plenty of daylight left. I sent a man ahead to get you a room at the Vista Bonita Hotel under the Arriaga Rim. The views are magnificent looking out over the timber country," said Verdugo. "It's the perfect spot for a honeymoon."

The forest country rose quickly to a height of about five thousand feet and was covered with ponderosa pine trees. The Arriaga Rim was a long escarpment that rose another two thousand feet straight up and was about fifty miles in length. The average elevation along this undulating rim was seven thousand feet.

"My new rancho near the international border is named Vista Bonita," Montoya told Verdugo. "I guess we are meant to stay there." An hour later, the newlyweds set off in a coach with their horses tied behind, with two vaqueros riding on top of the carriage.

Within four hours they reached the main lodge with its rustic looking log cabins spread out for more than one hundred yards. Each had views of the gorgeous forests spread for miles below the resort. Behind the main building was the two thousand foot high escarpment, jagged with irregular lines, cliffs, and boulder formations. The giant, slanting escarpment of volcanic and sedimentary rock was named "The Rock Monster" by local Mexicans.

Neither Christina nor Ricardo had ever seen anything like the beautiful forests, rock formations, and cliffs that surrounded them. They gazed down at the pine trees flowing out from the resort hotel, a deep green ocean that rippled softly over the landscape.

"This is a wonderful place for our honeymoon night," she told Ricardo. "Think of what it would be like to stand on top of the escarpment and look out at the horizon." Montoya had other ideas in mind as he passionately kissed his wife.

CHAPTER 25

Miguel Soto and ten riders arrived in Chihuahua an hour before dusk. He sent men to several stables in the community to find out if Ricardo and Christina had been seen. Soto's men flashed handfuls of money in exchange for news about the couple and their whereabouts, and got lucky at their third stop. A stable worker's eyes lighted up at the thought of making easy money, and explained that a carriage had been rented and was taking a tall man and a beautiful woman to the Hotel Vista Bonita in the timber country below the Arriaga Rim. The stable hand told them that it was about a half day's journey, and explained where the turn off to the hotel was located. Soto and his men ate dinner, traded their tired mounts for fresh horses, and set out on the trip to the hotel under the rim. They camped in the trees a quarter mile from the hotel and rested for a few hours.

***

Christina and Ricardo got up the next morning, had breakfast served in their room inside the main hotel building, and prepared to depart.

"Are you sure we can't stay a day or two longer?" she

asked. "This setting is absolutely beautiful."

Ricardo's mind was beginning to return to normal after the shock of the marriage. The blissful numbness of a newlywed husband's mind was suddenly swept aside by the need to protect Christina. "I'm sorry, Christina, but we have to go. There are people hunting us, and we need to stay ahead of them."

Ricardo and Christina walked out to the coach hand in hand, oblivious to their surroundings as they talked softly and laughed. A barrage of rifle fire erupted, exploding the early morning silence of the forest. Both vaqueros atop the coach were thrown off by the force of the bullets striking them in the head and chest, their bodies falling off both sides of the coach. Ricardo and Christina were partially shielded by the coach as bullets flew around them, knocking chunks of wood from the carriage.

Ricardo grabbed her arm and pulled Christina after him as he raced around the corner of the main hotel building, his wife in one hand and his rifle in the other. They ran to the back of the log building and fled down the hillside behind the structure and into the trees. "Keep your head down!" he told her.

Two gunmen came running around the corner of the building, and Montoya's first shot struck one man in the chest, knocking him to the ground. The second assassin fired his rifle, and the bullet struck the tree next to Ricardo. Montoya fired two more quick shots, and the gunman stopped running, a shocked expression on his face as he realized he had taken a rifle slug in the stomach. He sat down, wide-eyed, and then slumped over on his side. Montoya could hear Soto yelling to his men to charge forward. Ricardo grabbed Christina's arm again and pulled her after him as they ran downhill into a ravine, and along the bottom to a trail that worked its way upward, circling the hotel property.

"Where are we going?" she shouted.

"We need to get higher so we can fire down on our pursuers. Whoever has the high ground has the advantage." They continued to climb and crossed over several additional trails created by lodgers over time. The pair continued the upward climb until Christina was exhausted and slumped down behind a large rock outcropping. After a short rest, they began climbing again. The blanket of trees thinned out as they reached the main trail, which became a series of switchbacks as it progressed upward at steep angles. Ricardo reloaded his rifle and waited while Christina sat down again to catch her breath.

***

The group of assassins came together and turned the corner of the log building just as the two lead gunmen were downed by Montoya's gunfire. They stopped and moved backwards behind the hotel for protection. "Get going! Get after them!" Soto shouted. After a few moments the hired gunmen began running forward when they realized Ricardo and Christina were nowhere in sight. The pursuers became confused when they encountered crisscrossing trails...some ran one way, others took different paths.

***

When the first gunman came into full view, Ricardo shot him through the chest, causing him to tumble back down the slope.

"Let's go," he told Christina. The trail was relatively smooth from generations of people climbing the escarpment, and Christina was able to negotiate two switchbacks before she felt exhausted and had to rest. Ricardo was breathing heavily, but possessed a savage determination to protect his wife. His eyes were mere slits, teeth clenched together as he waited for the next target to appear.

***

"Keep climbing. Keep climbing," Soto yelled.

However, the pursuing gunmen were more careful now, having lost three of their own. They made no effort to move rapidly into open areas, and began studying the rocks and curvature of the trail before proceeding upward.

"See that switchback up ahead?" Soto said, and pointed. "When they make that turn on the switchback they will be open to rifle fire, so get ready!"

Eight rifles pointed at the location, but the pursuers were sweating and breathing heavily, keeping them from aiming properly. Rifle barrels moved slightly as the men gasped for breath.

***

Ricardo and Christina made the switchback turn, and both became visible for several seconds. Rifle fire rang out and bullets whizzed around the pair, sounding like angry bees. One bullet went through the brim of Ricardo's sombrero, and another grazed his shoulder. Christina was a much smaller target and no bullets came close. Ricardo pulled her around the corner of the switchback, and she slumped down behind a boulder.

"Climb to the next switchback, but don't make the turn until I tell you to!" he ordered.

She did as instructed, gasping for breath as the high altitude began to sap her remaining energy. Christina looked below at Ricardo, who was preparing to fire at the oncoming gunmen, and felt anxiety and apprehension begin to lessen. "Why am I not afraid?" she said aloud. "Something about

Ricardo gives me strength."

Montoya looked down the barrel of his rifle and squeezed off another shot as the lead gunmen turned the corner of a switchback. The assassin took a bullet through the head, his body pitched over the side of the trail, rolling him head over heels downward, starting a small avalanche of rocks and dirt. The other gunmen flattened themselves against the side of the rock wall.

"Keep moving! Don't stop!" Soto yelled. But the group had now lost four of their number, and fear mixed with caution kept them from moving upward. Soto began climbing again and came into view for a moment. Montoya recognized his black sombrero and matching black pants and vest as he fired, but Soto moved forward and out of sight too quickly, and the bullet struck the rock wall. Soto urged his men forward. "Come on! We're catching them! The man who shoots Montoya gets a ten thousand peso bonus!"

Ricardo stopped at a location where he had a clear, open shot at anyone in pursuit. "Christina, you climb as far and as fast as you can. They can't get past this spot. I'll start to climb once you're within a short distance of the summit." He handed her his revolver and she put it in the pocket of her leather skirt.

"I'll wave my hat to you when I reach the switchback over there," she said, and pointed upward to a location near the top of the escarpment. They embraced, and neither one wanted to let the other leave.

***

Soto discovered another trail that branched off to one side, and reasoned that it took a different route to the top. "Poncho! You and I will take this trail. The rest of you, continue upward."

The main group of gunmen halted for a few minutes to

rest and drink water from their canteens. They looked upward, studying the spot where they last saw Ricardo, but had no desire to begin their ascent again.

"I'm not going to die climbing this trail," one of the men snarled. "Let Soto do it!" The pursuit ground to a halt, and one by one the gunmen started back down the trail, self-preservation winning out over their desire for money.

**

Ricardo saw Christina waving her hat and began climbing. Both were exhausted, physically and mentally, by the time he reached her. "Give me a moment to rest, and we can get to the top," he said in a determined voice. Ten minutes later they reached the summit just as storm clouds moved in and sprayed them with a fine mist. Clouds obliterated everything for a few minutes, then passed through and visibility returned.

"Stay here for a minute while I check to see which direction we should go," Montoya said quietly

He moved off to the right and disappeared as another cloud came through, and the mist obliterated everything. Christina stood waiting for him to return in absolute silence, except for water softly dripping from the trees and bushes. The surreal atmosphere burst suddenly as two quick shots were fired. As the mist parted, a tall, thin Mexican appeared in front of Ricardo, an astonished look on his face. The assassin raised his revolver just as Montoya shot him in the heart. The gunman's revolver also fired, but the shot went wild.

**

Clouds passed through and visibility suddenly returned for Christina. Standing in front of her was Miguel Soto. Both of them stared at each other, startled looks on their faces, both antagonists momentarily frozen in time. A look of hatred flashed across Miguel's face, his eyes narrowed and his features reflected loathing and disgust.

"I am going to kill you slowly and with great pleasure," Soto snarled. He pulled his knife from its sheath and took a step towards her, growling like an animal, consumed with the desire to kill.

Christina reached into her skirt pocket, withdrew the revolver Ricardo had given her, and pointed it at his chest. "Don't come any closer," she warned him.

Soto smiled. "You haven't got the guts, you rotten bitch! I'm going to skin you alive!" he declared loudly.

Miguel raised his knife and Christina fired at point blank range, the slug striking him in the center of his chest. A look of astonishment and bewilderment passed over his features as he dropped to his knees. His mouth fell open and a dumbfounded look was frozen on his face. Wide-eyed, he tried to speak but no words came from his mouth.

Montoya came running up to them, and Soto shifted his gaze to Ricardo. "You bastard," he sputtered. Ricardo raised his rifle and fired. Soto cried out like a wounded animal, and his face twisted and jerked as he fell forward, dead.

Christina threw her arms around Ricardo. "Is it over?"

"Yes, it's finished."

They walked to the edge of the cliff, holding each other tightly as the clouds parted and the forest greenery was illuminated by the sun, signaling a new beginning. Ricardo kissed her tenderly, and they stood transfixed in the sunlight, staring down upon the green forest below, shimmering from the rain.

"Our life has just begun," he assured her. "I'll never let you go."

The End

Now Available

Before You Go...

HELP AN AUTHOR

write a review

THANK YOU!

Share your voice and help guide other readers to these wonderful books. Even if it's only a line or two your reviews help readers discover the author's books so they can continue creating stories that you'll love. Login to your favorite retailer and leave a review. Thank you

About the Author

Following college at The University of Missouri and a stint in the U. A. Army, Lee began a 15-year newspaper career at The Phoenix Gazette in Phoenix, Arizona. He wrote more than two thousand news articles and feature stories for The Gazette.

His main work emphasis was government and politics, and most of his career was spent writing about the Arizona State Capitol, the Arizona House of Representatives and the State Senate. Lee also covered the Phoenix City Council and Maricopa County governmental issues. He wrote numerous stories about prominent Arizona politicians including U. S. Senator Barry Goldwater, Speaker of the U. S. House of Representatives John Rhodes, and U. S. Senator Paul Fannin.

Lee had three novels published during and after his newspaper career, including Gunblaze by Leisure Books; the first book in the Border Legend series by Walker and Company, and Davy Crockett for Dell's American Explorers series.

He left the newspaper business to pursue a career in real estate and still owns a real estate company, Southwestern Homes Realty, in Scottsdale, Arizona.

Lee and his wife, Sue, have two sons and two daughters, who all live in the Phoenix and Tucson areas with their families. They have eight grand-children.

He is an avid outdoorsman who walks his boxers two to three miles each morning. Lee's favorite passion is hiking the Grand Canyon at least once a year. He also plays golf regularly.

Lee has returned to writing novels on a full-time basis and concentrates on southwestern historical fiction with action and adventure being the dominant focus.

He and his wife continue to reside in Scottsdale, Arizona.

www.ingramcontent.com/pod-product-compliance
Lightning Source LLC
Chambersburg PA
CBHW030252200626
46816CB00002BA/613